A new song ca
Wes grabbed h
me."

"Oh, but I—"

"No buts." He winked at Jim. "Nice meeting you."
He tugged Jillian toward the dance floor.

"That was rude."

"No," he said, spinning her around to face him.
"What was rude was the way you told me to get lost
last week."

"I did not."

He held her too closely, and as it always did when
he touched her the electricity that stretched
between them danced along his arms and his belly.
It'd been weeks since they'd been together, and yet
he still craved her just as badly as that first time.

"You did, and you've been avoiding me this week."
He felt her tense in his arms. "My mom says she's
asked you to come over at least a half a dozen
times."

"I've been busy."

"You've been avoiding me," he repeated.

Just as quickly as it'd come, the tension left her
body. "All right, I have."

Dear Reader,

Two years ago I bought a horse out of someone's backyard. It was love at first sight. It was almost a disaster.

The horse had serious mental issues. I feared for my life every day I went out to ride. If he wasn't trying to take my head off in his stall, he tried to kick me or run me down. Scary.

The breeder of the horse heard about my problems. She took pity on me and arranged for a session with a world-renowned animal communicator. Desperate, I agreed to talk to the communicator even though I didn't believe anyone could actually communicate with animals, especially over a phone. Boy, was I in for a surprise.

The communicator told me things about my horse that blew my mind, things that only I would know. She knew he had a problem with his right front hoof (he'd recently suffered an abscess). That he hated anyone invading his space. That he thought of himself as king. Most surprising of all, she claimed that he loved me. Loved? The skeptic in me had a hard time believing that. Still, I was desperate enough to listen to her advice.

Two months later it was like I owned a different horse. I became a believer.

There are things in life that we can't understand. I wanted to write about those things. I wanted to tell the story of a heroine with a heart as big as the animals she loved, but who was afraid. And I wanted to give her the man of her dreams—her perfect match. She just has to take her own advice—to trust in something you can't see—in this instance, love.

I hope you enjoy *Kissed by a Cowboy*.

Pamela

PS: To view pictures of my reformed rake of a horse visit my Facebook page at facebook.com/pamelabrittonauthor.

KISSED BY A COWBOY

Pamela Britton

HARLEQUIN® AMERICAN ROMANCE®

Recycling programs
for this product may
not exist in your area.

ISBN-13: 978-0-373-75557-8

Kissed by a Cowboy

Copyright © 2015 by Pamela Britton

All rights reserved. Except for use in any review, the reproduction or
utilization of this work in whole or in part in any form by any electronic,
mechanical or other means, now known or hereinafter invented, including
xerography, photocopying and recording, or in any information storage
or retrieval system, is forbidden without the written permission of the
publisher, Harlequin Enterprises Limited, 225 Duncan Mill Road,
Don Mills, Ontario M3B 3K9, Canada.

This is a work of fiction. Names, characters, places and incidents are
either the product of the author's imagination or are used fictitiously,
and any resemblance to actual persons, living or dead, business
establishments, events or locales is entirely coincidental.

This edition published by arrangement with Harlequin Books S.A.

For questions and comments about the quality of this book,
please contact us at CustomerService@Harlequin.com.

® and TM are trademarks of Harlequin Enterprises Limited or its
corporate affiliates. Trademarks indicated with ® are registered in the
United States Patent and Trademark Office, the Canadian Intellectual
Property Office and in other countries.

Printed in U.S.A.

With over a million books in print, **Pamela Britton** likes to call herself the best-known author nobody's ever heard of. Of course, that changed thanks to a certain licensing agreement with that little racing organization known as NASCAR.

But before the glitz and glamour of NASCAR, Pamela wrote books that were frequently voted the best of the best by the *Detroit Free Press*, Barnes & Noble (two years in a row) and *RT Book Reviews*. She's won numerous awards, including a National Readers' Choice Award and a nomination for the Romance Writers of America Golden Heart® Award.

When not writing books, Pamela is a reporter for a local newspaper. She's also a columnist for the *American Quarter Horse Journal*.

Books by Pamela Britton

Harlequin American Romance

Cowboy Lessons
Cowboy Trouble
Cowboy M.D.
Cowboy Vet
Cowgirl's CEO
The Wrangler
Mark: Secret Cowboy
Rancher and Protector
The Rancher's Bride
A Cowboy's Pride
A Cowboy's Christmas Wedding
A Cowboy's Angel
The Texan's Twins

Harlequin HQN

Dangerous Curves
In the Groove
On the Edge
To the Limit
Total Control
On the Move

Visit the Author Profile page at Harlequin.com for more titles.

In Memory

Colonels Smoking Gun

(Gunner)

1993–2013

Chapter One

"Not that one."

Wesley Landon glanced at the woman who'd spoken. Who was she talking to? With her friendly smile and bright blue eyes, she had to be the prettiest thing he'd seen all day. Then again, there were half a dozen people lining the rail at the 51st Annual Red Bluff Bull and Gelding Sale. Clearly, though, she'd been speaking to someone inside the arena.

"Can you lope him out a bit?" he called to the kid who owned the gelding he was considering purchasing.

"Sure thing," the young man answered as he urged the big bay into a slow run.

The horse sure had the looks, Wes thought, his heart pumping in tempo with his mounting excitement. "What do you think, Cowboy? You think he's the one?"

The border collie glanced up at him and wagged his tail, his bright brown gaze declaring he was far more thrilled to look into his owner's eyes than at the horse in question.

"Well, I think he is," Wes said. If the gelding didn't turn into a total nutcase during the competition portion of the sale, he might have found a diamond in the rough.

"Seriously." Out of the corner of his eye, he saw the woman edge closer. "That horse is plumb crazy."

Wes glanced left again, surprised to see the cute little brunette staring at him. So she *was* talking to him.

"Excuse me?"

"The horse you're looking at."

She wasn't flirting, he realized in disappointment—she was trying to psych him out. It wasn't uncommon for the competition to do that. Sometimes they would tell out-and-out lies in the hopes of souring a sale.

"Who told you that?" he said, playing along.

She smiled. She had a nose that was tipped up at the end and when she grinned, the smile lit up her face and her bright green eyes like the dawn of sunrise. In a light blue ribbed shirt—one the same color as the California sky above—and jeans tucked into fancy cowboy boots, she didn't look like someone who'd tell a lie. She looked innocent and sweet and, yes, beautiful.

"The horse did."

"Excuse me?" he said again.

"What's your dog's name?" She came forward, smiling down now.

"Cowboy."

"Hey, Cowboy." She knelt, scratching the dog under his white chin before she rested her forehead on his black mask. "How are you, gorgeous?"

Okay, there was something about a woman loving on his dog that never failed to soften Wes's mood, even if she *was* trying to pull the wool over his eyes. Unless maybe he'd misunderstood her.

"Did you *see* him buck someone off?"

She stood. "Nope. I can just tell by looking at him."

Okay, this was ridiculous. He held back his laughter, although just barely. "You can just tell," he asked, wanting to be absolutely clear. "By looking at him."

A nod, one that set her angular bob—her hair more black than brown—into motion. It brushed her jawline, that hair, coming to a point by her chin. Wes was struck by the notion that the cut perfectly accentuated her pixielike face. A face filled with utter seriousness.

His smile faltered. "I think you might be wrong about this one." He glanced back at the animal in question. The gelding loped around like a pleasure pony, completely calm and relaxed.

She shrugged. "Suit yourself." She shifted her smile down to his dog. "Nice talking to you, Cowboy."

He watched her leave, admitting he'd never seen such light green eyes; her gaze seemed otherworldly, and it tried to convince him she told the truth. He didn't believe her, of course. There might be some people who could take one look at a horse and know if it was a good animal, but he'd never met any. His friend Zach knew someone like that. A friend of his fiancée's. He claimed she was a real-life horse whisperer, a woman with short black hair and bright—

He jerked around. "Jillian?"

She immediately turned and frowned. "Yes?"

Oh, good Lord. This was one of Zach's fiancée's best friends, the horse trainer.

"You're Jillian Thacker?"

She smiled a bit, and he could tell the grin was tinged with relief. "Oh, good, maybe now he'll believe me " relief. She tipped her head.

"Do I know you?"

"No. Yes. Sort of. I'm Wes Landon."

Any doubt that she didn't recognize the name faded

the moment he saw her green eyes widen almost imperceptibly. Her gaze swept over him as if matching up her last image of him—probably out at Golden Downs racetrack—with the man in the cowboy hat, long-sleeved white button-down, jeans and boots who stood before her. He'd seen her before, too; he just hadn't recognized her.

"Well, well, well," she said, her eyes narrowing before she slowly crossed her arms. "The evil racehorse owner in the flesh."

He smiled, well aware of her derision but completely unfazed. He knew that she and her fellow members of CEASE—Concerned Equestrians Aiding in Saving Equines—hated him. Okay, not really hated, more like…wanted to put him out of a job. They couldn't stand people who raced horses, because they all thought it was cruel. It still struck him as a small miracle that Zach had somehow managed to charm the founder of the group, Mariah Stewart, into marrying him.

"Well, well, well, if it isn't Dr. Dolittle in the flesh."

Zach had taken to calling her that. When Wes had first heard about the woman who claimed to have a special touch with horses, he'd pretended to believe it was possible. He didn't, of course. In his line of work as an equine-farm manager he'd heard it all. The miracle worker who could pop a horse's bones into place and make them instantly sound. The massage therapist for sore equines. The herbal concoction that would give a horse extra zip. It wasn't that he didn't believe some of that stuff might help—he just wasn't sold they were the miracles some people purported them to be.

"What are you doing here?" She lifted a brow. "Slumming it?"

"I could ask the same of you."

He'd only ever seen her from a distance, usually as he was driving through the entrance of Golden Downs racetrack, and she was holding a protest sign. Cute, he admitted, even if she *was* bat-shit crazy.

"I'm here with a client. She had me look at that one yesterday."

They both turned to stare at the horse in question. "Given your low opinion of me, I'm surprised you didn't encourage me to buy him."

She released a huff of agreement. "Even if I *had* recognized you, and I might not like what you do for a living, that doesn't mean I want to see you get killed, either."

"Ah, but see, I don't make my living racing horses."

"Yeah, right. I've seen you at Golden Downs. You're the owner of Landon Farms."

He took pleasure in contradicting her. "My *mom* owns Landon Farms. I just manage her operation, so technically, my mom's the enemy." He gave her a teasing smile. "So if you like, I can give you her cell phone number so you can call her and tell her how much you despise what she does for a living."

She appeared genuinely perplexed. He wasn't surprised. It was a common misconception that he was part owner. "But you're always at the track."

"Not always." He met the gaze of the cowboy riding the gelding and signaled him to stop. "I drop horses off and sometimes pop in to see my mom, but that's about it. Racing is my mom's thing."

"But…Mariah told me you're on the board of directors at Golden Downs."

"Because of my mom." The seat had actually been

foisted on him by both his mom and his fellow board members, sort of a consolation prize back when his dad had died. As if a board seat could make up for his loss. "She insists I keep my finger on the pulse of the industry, for her sake."

A look of curiosity had taken the place of her frown. She glanced at the horse in the arena, then back at him. "So what are you doing here, Mr. Farm Manager?"

"Looking for my next cutting horse." But as he thought about the *reason* he was looking, his stomach soured.

Ah, ah, ah. Don't go there.

"I ride and train cutting horses out of my mom's farm."

He waited for yet another look of derision, but she apparently didn't mind that type of horse competition, because she nodded.

"We're looking for a reining prospect. My friend Natalie decided she'd like to give it a try—goodness knows why. As if jumping horses doesn't keep her busy enough."

Natalie Goodman—he'd heard of her thanks to Mariah. It seemed as though everyone knew everybody in the small town of Via Del Caballo, especially if you were into horses.

"So what makes you think there's something wrong with this horse?" He might not believe in her "special touch," but he was curious.

"I can just tell by looking at him."

"Uh-huh."

Clearly she'd picked up on his skepticism. "If you look closely enough, you can see it in his eyes."

They both eyed the horse. "All I see is an animal doing its job."

"Right now, yes, but look at the way its tail is twitching, a sure sign it's bothered by something." She pointed, her expression one of complete conviction. "Every time that cowboy asks him to do something, he twitches. He doesn't do anything about it now, because he's too tired, but I can tell that horse would ordinarily blow, its rider tossed to the ground in the process."

He scratched his chin absently, although maybe not so absently, because he noticed he needed to shave. "Let me get this straight. You think because that horse's tail is twitching that it wants to buck that cowboy off?"

"Yup. And look at its ears. And the way its nose is wrinkled. Classic signs of a horse that's not happy doing its job."

He had to admit, she had a point. "And so based on that you think he's a nut."

She shook her head. "No. That's just what tipped me off he might be a nut. I spotted him yesterday, thought he looked nice, so I peeked in on him last night, and he damn near took my head off the moment I opened his stall door. I actually heard his teeth clack together when he tried to bite me." She shivered. "Scary."

He didn't know what to say, didn't know if he should make a pithy comment of his own or if he should pretend as if he believed her.

"I slammed the door just in time. He kicked it just in case I didn't get the message. Bam!" She reenacted the moment by pretending to jump, her bob swinging. "Scared me half to death."

He glanced back at the horse, although he did so to get control of his facial expressions. Was she trying to sour him on a sale? She didn't look like the deceptive type. The docile-looking gelding didn't look like a nut, either. It walked with its head down, ears pricked forward now, eyes bright—completely contradicting her claims.

"Bring him outside, if you don't mind," he called to the man riding him, though why he did so he had no idea.

The horse obeyed the rider instantly. Wes shot Jillian an expression of doubt. As good-looking horses went, the gelding took the cake. A little taller than he would like for a potential cutting horse, perhaps, but he'd seen some bigger geldings get down in the dirt. He'd watched a video of him working cows yesterday and been impressed. If he'd owned the horse, he wouldn't have offered him for sale for any amount of money.

He eyed the man on horseback, a younger cowboy with scruffy blond hair who hadn't outgrown acne just yet. "You the owner?"

The kid's eyes darted right before he answered, "Yes," but the way he said the one word caught Wes's attention. A little too quick. Wes might have missed it if he hadn't been listening closely.

"How long have you had him?"

Again the cagey look. "Long enough to know he's a good one."

Honestly, he didn't believe Jillian was some kind of horse whisperer, but he didn't like the way the kid was responding to his questions, either. "Ever been bucked off him?"

If he'd looked uncomfortable before, he was positively sitting on tacks now. "No, sir."

"Never?"

"Wellll, he can get a little high sometimes, but nothing someone with a good seat can't handle."

Wes had heard enough. "Okay, then. Thanks for showing him to me. I appreciate it."

He turned away before he said something sarcastic. Cowboy fell into step beside him. Good Lord, the kid was a bad liar. He heard more than saw Jillian follow in his wake.

"Now, there's a horse trader if ever I've seen one," she said.

Horse trader. The scourge of the equine industry. People who picked up horses for cheap and tried to resell them, usually telling a whole boatload of lies along the way. He would bet if he looked at the horse's registration papers, he'd see that the kid wasn't even listed as owner. He stopped suddenly.

"Did you see him try to buck that kid off earlier?"

Jillian drew back, obviously offended. "No. I told you, I could tell something was off the moment I spotted him and so I dropped in on him last night."

He looked away from her piercing green eyes, still not really convinced, but damned if he didn't agree that something wasn't right. Perhaps it'd been a lucky guess on her part.

"You believe me now, don't you?"

He faced her squarely. "I believe you're an astute horsewoman, one smart enough to check up on a prospect when nobody was around. And I believe you're probably right. If he's got issues in the stall, he probably has issues under saddle."

"Thank you. I'm flattered."

They stood in a place just outside the arena, in between the fenced enclosure and a long line of stalls.

Horse heads bobbed up and down as they watched the activity directly across from them.

"I don't know why you men are always such skeptics," she added. "I get so tired of having to explain to your sex why I feel a certain way about a horse. For once it'd be nice to meet someone who says, 'Oh, you have a gut feeling? I completely understand. Thanks for the tip.'"

A horse neighed in the distance. In the arena, one of the animals being ridden answered back. Typical sounds for an equine event except in the distance, off in the barns a ways away, one could hear the sounds of bulls calling to each other. Wes had planned to go look at them earlier, but then he'd spotted the kid riding the gelding...

He turned back to Jillian. She sure was cute, especially standing there, branches from a nearby tree sifting sunlight onto her hair and throwing dappled patterns on her shoulders.

"I see your point, and I'm glad you spoke up. I'm still interested in the horse, but I'll be watching him more closely from here on out."

"Suit yourself, but I'm telling you, you'll be sorry if you end up buying him." She bent and scratched Cowboy again.

"Duly noted."

"Your dog knows I'm right, too."

"Yeah?" Cowboy whined. When Wes looked down, he was chagrined to realize his dog sat at Jillian's feet.

"Dogs have a sixth sense about other animals. They know when they're bad. You ever watch a cattle dog run up to the rankest bull in the herd? They just know, and they step in to protect their master."

"If you say so."

"One more thing," she said. "If you want your dog to stop chewing your boots, give him something else— like a pig ear or a cow bone. He's never going to stop on his own."

Wes jerked upright.

"What makes you think he likes to chew my boots?"

"Another gut feeling."

He didn't move for a second. Could she see the chew marks along the top? No, she couldn't see them.

"Lucky guess."

She must have realized she wasn't going to get anywhere with him, because she nodded. "Just do me a favor. Stay away from that horse. He's a bad one."

"Duly noted."

She turned away. He watched her for a moment before doing the same. Crazy. The whole thing was crazy.

"By the way," he heard her call, "Cowboy strikes me as the type that likes to bury things, so if you're missing a boot, check for fresh piles of dirt."

He almost stumbled. She was looking over her shoulder, a wicked smile on her face. How did she know about *that*—?

She started walking backward, thumbs hooked in her jeans. "But that was probably just a lucky guess, too, huh?"

She turned away before he could respond, which was probably a good thing because she'd done something a woman hadn't done to him in a long time.

She'd rendered him completely speechless.

Chapter Two

Typical male, Jillian thought as she took her time walking back to the show arena. You had to slap them in the face with the truth before they believed you.

Story of her life.

If he had a hard time believing she had a sixth sense, then he'd *really* freak out when he discovered the truth. Still, he'd seemed nice, she thought as she reached the interior of the massive enclosed arena, the sound of Gene Robertson, this year's clinician, droning on in the background. Oh, damn. She'd wanted to watch that. That was what she got for dillydallying outside.

"There you are," said one of her closest friends, Natalie Goodman, a blonde spitfire who had every cowboy within twenty yards looking their way. Thanks to her trim figure, bright blue eyes and generous smile, men didn't know what hit them when she looked in their direction.

"I was out talking to Wes Landon." She took a seat on the aluminum bleachers that stretched along one side of the arena. Her backside instantly chilled. It was the end of January and if you weren't out in the sunlight, you froze half to death.

"Landon, Landon," Natalie was saying. "Why does that name sound so familiar?"

"Zach's friend. The one who races horses, only he tells me he isn't the one who breeds them or owns them. He just manages his mom's farm."

"*That* Wes," Natalie said, focusing on the man on horseback. He spoke about the shape of a horse's shoulder and its importance when it came to clearing obstacles, something that Natalie should have been speaking to the crowd about. Natalie was a shoo-in for this year's equestrian games in show jumping. As long as they could keep her primary mount, Nero, sound, she'd be representing the United States of America.

"Was he as good-looking as Mariah claims?"

"He's not bad."

More like drop-dead gorgeous with his blond hair and green eyes. He had the looks of a movie star. She frowned because that was something she knew first-hand.

Negative energy. Focus on the positive.

"Not bad?" Natalie repeated, blond brow arched over an almond-shaped eye.

"Okay, fine. He's pretty hot."

No sense in denying it. Natalie would see for herself one day soon.

"Wow, that's pretty high praise coming from a woman who dated Jason Brown."

"Shh," she hissed, glancing around. She had no idea why. It wasn't as if there were members of the paparazzi nearby. Those days were long behind her.

"What? I think it's kind of cool that you dated *People* magazine's sexiest man alive."

"Yeah, well, they didn't know him like I did."

He'd called her because he'd been having problems with his Arabian stallion. She should have known right then that he was an idiot because only egotistical jerks owned stallions if they weren't in the breeding business. But no, she'd accepted the job, figured out the problem and ended up getting asked out on a date, and he was just so dang handsome and sweet that she'd said yes. And then yes again. Only he'd turned out to be nothing like the men he portrayed on-screen. He wasn't a sweetly sexy hometown boy. He was an ass who'd broken her heart.

"…don't you think?"

Jillian shook her head. That was all in the past. A long time ago, in a galaxy far, far away…

"What?" she had to ask.

"I said you should probably answer your cell phone, don't you think?"

Jillian jumped, then fished into her back pocket for her phone and as she glanced down at the unfamiliar number, she knew—she just knew.

"It's him."

Sometimes her abilities extended beyond the animal kingdom.

"Him who?"

"Wes Landon."

Natalie smirked. "That was quick."

"Yeah."

She ignored the voice of reason, the one that told her to ignore him because he was just a little too good-looking. It would be easy to forget the rules around him.

Her finger had a mind of its own. "Hello?"

"You ran away before you could give me your phone number."

She wanted to grin like a silly teenage girl. *What a doofus.* She had sworn off men after Jason had left her shattered.

She glanced left. Natalie stared, her expression one of clear interest.

"You never indicated you wanted it," she admitted. "Not that I was surprised. You know, me being a crazy woman and all."

Next to her, Natalie broke into a wide smile.

"Come to think of it, how *did* you get my number?"

"Mariah."

"I should have known."

She shot Natalie a look of apology and then stood, heading toward the middle of the building and the exit. She didn't need grief from her friend.

"What did you want?" she asked.

The noise of the crowd in the arena made it hard to hear and so she headed for the atrium at the front of the building. The smell of hot dogs and hamburgers filled the air and reminded her she hadn't eaten lunch.

"You were right." There was a pause, and she could perfectly imagine him shaking his head. Or maybe that was a visual she picked up from his dog. Hard to tell.

"I followed that horse back to the barn so I could watch the kid untack."

"Oh?" She'd reached the exit and it was immediately quieter. "What'd you find out?"

A large man with a dog at his side blocked her path. The dog was a black-and-white border collie. She glanced up sharply, her heart flipping over in her chest. Beautiful green eyes smiled down at her from beneath a black cowboy hat, one nearly as dark as the man's lashes.

"He about kicked the kid in the head."

Her hand dropped, cell phone forgotten. His hand did the same, although he took the time to disconnect. She absently did the same.

"And then he yelled, 'You crazy son of a bitch,' before he spotted me standing there."

Hey, Cowboy, she silently telegraphed the dog. A long black tail started to wag. She smiled and returned her attention to Wes.

So handsome. So ridiculously gorgeous. Mariah had been trying to set him up with one of the girls from the barn for ages, and he was so cute she might have been tempted to throw caution to the wind if they'd been introduced before now...before she'd pegged him as a doubting Thomas.

"Did he get nailed?" she asked to cover that particularly troubling thought.

Green eyes sparked. "Nah. He's fine." She saw his lips turn up in a brief smile as he remembered the incident. "But when he realized I'd heard, I could tell he was about to offer up some excuse. I told him don't bother."

"So you believe me now?"

And why did the thought make her so giddy? She knew what his answer would be even though she hoped for something different.

"I believe you intuitively knew something was off with that gelding."

Intuition. A sixth sense. Men had excused her abilities a million times over. Women had, too, but it always felt different when it was a man.

"I'm usually pretty good at reading horses, but I'll admit I missed the mark on this one."

"That's big of you."

His smile was pure charm. "Mariah says you're the real deal, a bona fide horse whisperer, and so I was thinking…"

No. Don't say it. She didn't want to spend any more time with him. To be honest, she had been glad when he let her walk away.

"…maybe between the two of us…"

He didn't finish, but he didn't need to. She knew what he was thinking.

"You want me to help you pick out some prospects, don't you?"

"Yeah. Exactly."

She shouldn't have been surprised. Still, there was a part of her that wished that for once in her life she could meet someone and tell them the truth. It wasn't a sixth sense. She picked up images from the minds of animals. Her friend Mariah said she talked to them, but it wasn't really that. She could see what was going on in their minds, but she could never tell people that, not when she first met them. They'd call her crazy, but for some reason she wanted to tell Wes, and she wanted him to believe her.

It's because you think he's cute.

"What's in it for me?"

She hadn't meant the question to come out so cool, but something about the man set her teeth on edge. It was as if she fought an invisible force field, one she wanted to break through.

He doesn't believe you and that hurts.

It shouldn't have hurt. It never hurt. So why now?

"I don't know. What do you have in mind?"

You.

She almost blanched. "Money."

Beneath his black cowboy hat his brow lifted. "You mean like pay you for your services?"

"Something like that."

"How much are your rates?"

"I'm expensive, but I have another idea."

The brim of his cowboy hat tipped a bit. If she wasn't mistaken, his gaze had just intensified, green eyes flashing with...what? Interest?

"Like what?"

Good Lord, he'd taken her words wrong. He was thinking something personal. "I'll help you in exchange for a sizable donation to CEASE."

If she'd told him she wanted to use the money to fly to the moon, he couldn't have looked any more surprised.

"You're kidding."

"Nope. See, we want to hold a big fund-raiser, but we're a little short on cash. If you want my help, you'll have to help CEASE."

She heard him huff something out under his breath. He wouldn't accept, *couldn't* accept. She had a feeling the whole "you have a good eye" thing was just an excuse to get to know her better. Chances were, as a farm manager, he had a good eye, too. He didn't need her. Not really, but she could tell her offer had put him off. He might not breed horses, but she knew he didn't like the group she hung out with; ergo, he wouldn't like her... or so she'd thought. The dratted man actually appeared to be considering her offer.

Why had she ever opened her mouth about that horse?

Wes Landon could be dangerous to her health. Good-looking. Sexy smile. Horse lover. She'd never be able to resist his charms, and if she didn't, she'd pay the price once he discovered the truth about her "sixth sense." She always did.

"Let me get this straight." He leaned in closer to her. "You want me, a farm manager whose mother breeds racehorses, to donate money to CEASE, the people who picket the racetrack where my mom runs her horses."

"Yup."

Don't say yes. Don't say yes. Don't say yes.

But he didn't look as perturbed as she'd expected. "Deal."

God help her.

Chapter Three

The next day she was still irritated as hell that she'd agreed to help. Granted, it was for a good cause, but that didn't mean it wasn't going to be a pain in the rear. She'd had to spend all day yesterday visiting the horses in the sale catalog. Natalie had joined her, and Jillian had mulled over each horse, trying to decide if it would work best for Natalie or Wes.

Fortunately, she hunted for two very different animals. Reining horses performed a pattern in an arena, trotting, loping and running, followed by working with a cow. Cutting was all about the cow, so it was easy to separate the two types of horses. By the end of Wednesday she'd picked out a horse for Wes, but instead of being excited to see him, he stared at the animal as if she'd lost her mind.

"You've got to be kidding me," he said Thursday morning.

The thing about his opinion of the horse was that it didn't disturb her nearly as much as the man himself. There were times when you met a man and he just… did something to your insides. Wes was one of those men for Jillian. Frankly, he was probably "one of those men" for a lot of women. She'd seen women do double takes as she'd followed Wes over to the stables. She didn't blame them. He might have been wearing nothing more than jeans and a dark green button-down, but the cotton shirt did something to his eyes. They were so green you could spot them from ten paces away.

"Okay, I know he's not much to look at, but it's what's inside that counts," she said, referring to the horse they were examining.

"Is he even big enough to carry my weight?"

Jillian nodded her head emphatically. The horse looked as plain as a copper penny, she admitted. He stood in the far corner, head toward them, the smell of pine shavings in the air. His red coat marked him as a sorrel, and about the only thing interesting about his features was the blaze on his face. Typical of horses that traced back to the legendary Gunner, the white covered nearly half his head—the top half. Horse people called it bald-faced. Jillian called it a good sign—a sign he had a lot of his sire's blood in him.

"He's by Colonels Smoking Gun, Wes, one of reining's all-time leading sires."

"I know who he is."

"I think he's going to be just like him."

"But I don't *want* a reining horse."

"I know, I know. But he's cutting bred on the bottom. He's got Dual Rey in his lines. And he likes cows, and he has his father's desire to win."

He glanced at her sharply. "Let me guess. Another one of your 'feelings'?"

"Yes."

He eyed the gelding again. "He looks like a mule."

"He does not!"

Wes stepped back from the stall and crossed his

arms. The horse inside barely lifted his head. The gelding looked tired, Jillian noticed. She closed her eyes
for a brief moment and asked the question she didn't
want to ask.

You okay?

She received an image of long spurs and sweat-
soaked sides. Of an evil-looking spade bit and a dusty
arena. His owner had ridden the socks off him last night.

Poor baby.

The horse lifted its head, nodding as if in silent
agreement.

"What are you doing?"

Jillian's eyes popped open. She wasn't normally so
obvious, especially in front of men.

"Ahh. Nothing. Piece of sawdust in my eyes."

He turned to face her again. Beneath the overhang
of a stall he seemed all the more imposing. He wore
cowboy hats low on his brow, she noticed, not that it
mattered how he wore them, because he was a big man
and he probably could have covered his nose and still
seen the world.

"You okay?"

She looked down at Wes's feet, at the dog that faith-
fully sat by his side. *Your human is very handsome.*

The dog wagged his tail, the soft hairs brushing the
ground and kicking up dirt.

And he probably knows it, too.

"Fine." She nodded toward the horse. "See how quiet
he is?"

"Well, yeah, I don't need a sixth sense to know why
that is. Clearly someone rode him pretty hard today.
Look at the marks by his girth."

She leaned in, then immediately drew back. How

had she missed that? She could see where the skin was raised beneath the hide. Horizontal lines and one diagonal line intersected right about where a spur would rest. She would bet if she examined the gelding up close, she'd find broken skin.

"You have to buy him."

Cowboy whined as if trying to urge his master to do as she suggested, but she could tell Wes wasn't convinced.

"And why should I do that?"

"Look at him. Nice head, and with that short back, he ought to be pretty handy. He's flashy, too, with those four white socks and half-white head. And smart. You can tell by looking in his eyes."

"I don't like four white feet. Their hooves are horrible. Too brittle." Their gazes connected. "Sorry—I probably should have told you that before you started scouting prospects."

"You don't even want to see him work? Because of his feet?"

"I'm saying no because he's reining bred, too. He even looks like a reiner."

"Would you refuse to date a woman because she came from the wrong bloodlines?"

She had no idea where the question came from, except maybe she was trying to give herself one more reason to stop thinking about the breadth of his shoulders. Normally, she would never push a client toward something they didn't want, but she enjoyed the way his eyes widened beneath his black hat. She could practically hear the thoughts going through his head.

Should I answer that? Maybe I shouldn't. Lord, that's a loaded question.

She almost laughed.

"I guess it would depend on the woman."

"How about a woman who's short, a little bit over-weight, but who makes you laugh. Would you say no to that?"

Why was she pushing him?

"Well, I can overlook a lot of things if someone can cook." He smiled. She looked away. "How's your cook-ing?"

"I can't boil an egg," she lied.

She thought she heard him laugh. And she could have sworn he softly said, "Liar."

Okay, so she was a great cook, but she wasn't going to let the conversation flow into territory she'd rather avoid.

Arm's length, she reminded herself.

She'd agreed to help him because of CEASE, be-cause what they needed, what they had always needed, was a wealthy sponsor to help fund their organization. With financial backing they could get the word out, tell more people about the plight of unwanted racehorses. Not just racehorses but all horses. His mother might be just the ticket.

"Seriously, Wes, you shouldn't turn up your nose at something because it's different from what you want. Plenty of good reining horses have made good cutting horses—and vice versa."

Was she speaking to herself? Or him?

When she felt his gaze fall upon her, she dared to look up at him.

"That sounded personal."

It had been, and she had no idea why she'd said it, not after warning herself off.

"No. Not at all. I just think you should give him a try."

He went back to peering at the horse in the stall. So did she. Inside, the gelding swished his tail.

"He's young," Jillian added. "He'll do some growing over the next couple of years."

She felt something cold and wet touch her hand. When she glanced down, Cowboy stared up at her.

Maybe you can talk some sense into him.

More tail wagging.

"Okay, fine. I'll watch him perform today."

"Really?"

He nodded.

She didn't know why she did it, didn't have a clue what prompted her, but suddenly she hugged him. She felt so strongly about the gelding in the stall it took her breath away. She didn't pretend to be psychic. She just had a feeling they'd be a perfect match.

"Wow." He drew back. "If I'd known that'd be your reaction, I'd have said yes ten minutes ago."

She felt so small in his arms. Hated that she noticed again how wide his shoulders were. Loved the way his eyes lit up when he smiled.

She stepped back.

"Sorry. I just think…" *You have the sexiest eyes I've ever seen.* "You won't be disappointed."

She turned away before she forgot it all—forgot the pain and sorrow and wasted tears she'd spent on one man after another. Forgot the crushing disappointment and how stupid she felt afterward, forgot how many times she'd gotten her hopes up by telling herself, once again, that it would be different this time around.

It never was.

She started to turn away again.

"Wait."

She didn't turn back, didn't want to look him in the eyes. She didn't want to connect with him at all.

"Don't you have more for me to look at?"

"Nope." She gave him her profile. "He's it."

"Well, all right, then," he said. "What time do you want to hook up at the arena?"

"One o'clock. He's the third one out."

She didn't wait for him to respond. He would either be there or he wouldn't. From here on out it was horses and horsemanship. That was *it*.

Too bad she had a feeling it wouldn't be that easy.

Chapter Four

"She's an odd one, isn't she?"

Cowboy peered up at him intently.

And you're getting desperate, buddy, if you're talking to your dog.

A cute oddball, he amended, watching her walk away, but an oddball just the same.

Desperate straits call for desperate measures.

The words had become his mantra recently. If Bugsy hadn't pulled up lame... He shook his head in disgust and disappointment. Now he was dead in the water and a fully trained replacement horse would cost a fortune, which was why he'd traveled to Red Bluff this weekend to look at prospects. The equine equivalent to a Hail Mary pass. He had to find a horse that could nudge him over the half-million-dollar mark in earnings. Pronto. If he didn't... Well, he couldn't even think about that.

"Come on," he said to Cowboy.

Two hours later she stood right where she'd said she'd be, out in front of the two-story brown building that served as a horse arena. She wasn't alone. A woman with blond hair and blue eyes stood next to her.

"Wes," Jillian said, barely making eye contact. "This is Natalie."

He glanced at Natalie, offering a "Nice to meet you" before looking back at Jillian and puzzling through why she seemed so cold all of a sudden.

"Wow," he heard Natalie say. "You weren't kidding when you said he was good-looking."

He had a front-row seat to Jillian's reaction. She flinched, turned on her friend and sharply whispered, "Natalie!"

Now, that was more like it. At least she had some color back in her cheeks.

She thought he was good-looking?

For some reason that made him stand up a little straighter.

"And who's this cutie?" Natalie said.

"This is Cowboy," Wes said.

Natalie squatted down to meet his dog. "Hey there, boy. Gonna watch some horses work with us?"

Cowboy barely shot Natalie a glance. His dog only had eyes for Jillian. The canine stared at her as if she held the keys to a room filled with bones.

"We better get in there before the seats all fill up," Jillian said.

She still wouldn't look at him. It'd grown colder since that morning. Overcast. Both women wore jackets, Natalie's made of leather and Jillian's a black knitted cardigan that hung past her hips to midthigh. It hugged her petite body but didn't look all that warm, and he knew it would be even colder inside.

"Are you excited?" Natalie asked Wes.

"I'm curious," he replied. "The horse Jillian chose for me isn't exactly what I was looking for."

Natalie nodded. "I know how you feel. She narrowed the field down to three for me, and not a one of them is what I would have picked for myself. But I've learned over the years to listen to her. You'll learn the same thing, too."

Great, he thought as they headed inside. Two *crazy women*.

The building had been built in the '50s. A beige stucco facade on the outside and a concrete floor that seemed to radiate the chill. They were a little late to be finding a seat, most of the grandstands already filled, but they wedged themselves into a spot near the top. Cowboy settled at Wes's feet. It looked like a sea of cowboy hats from where they sat, as if you could hop from brim to brim and never touch the ground.

"I'm so excited," he heard Natalie say. She wore her long blond hair in a braid, a brown ball cap on her head, one with rhinestones in the shape of a horseshoe catching the light. The glimmer of the stones nearly matched the blue in her eyes. "I can't believe I'm actually doing this."

"Me neither," Jillian said, and Wes noticed she'd made sure Natalie sat next to him and that Jillian sat on the other side of Natalie—as far away as possible. "I have no idea how you're going to wedge in learning to ride a reining horse and continue with your show jumping career, too."

"Who's your reining trainer?" Wes asked.

"I don't have one."

Wes pulled his gaze away from a horse just entering the arena, an average-looking bay gelding with big ears and a bushy black tail, and shot her a look of surprise. "You're buying a reining horse and you don't have a trainer?"

"I am a trainer," Natalie said.

"You ride English."

"Yeah, which means I know how to ride." He tried to keep a straight face; clearly he failed. "You try and ride a horse over a five-foot fence."

"No, thanks, I prefer to keep my feet on the ground, but I know someone who would take up your challenge."

"Oh, yeah?"

"A friend of mine. A rodeo performer. I'll have to introduce the two of you."

"Rodeo?" Natalie's look said it all. *Yuck.* "Can't imagine anyone involved with the world of rodeo knowing anything about reining horses."

"You might be surprised."

In fact, he'd make a point of introducing the two. In the arena a black horse worked—unimpressively, he thought—over so-called trail obstacles that were nothing more than wood poles, tires and plastic bags filled with aluminum cans. The gelding was slow on the uptake, so much so he almost dumped his rider when the man picked up one of the bags.

"That was scary," he heard Jillian say.

The main arena had been sectioned off into three different pens. The first was meant to showcase the animal's horse sense—in this case, none. The second was for showing off the animal's maneuverability. The third was where they would work a cow. The middle ring was the one that Natalie would pay close attention to because that was where the horse would circle, stop and back…along with a few other tasks, all moves that would be necessary at a reining competition.

Less than a minute later a horn sounded, signaling it was time to move. Alas, the black horse didn't appear to be any better at reining than he was at trail. Meanwhile, a new horse had entered the first ring. There would always be a horse working in one of the pens, something that made watching interesting.

"Here we go," Jillian said. "This is one of the horses we're interested in."

Curiosity made him study the dark bay gelding. Like the horse Jillian had picked out for him, the gelding hardly seemed impressive. No flashy white on his face. No tiny dish head. No thick neck and round butt. He seemed as plain as a brown paper package. He glanced at the catalog. The horse's name was Playboy Gunslinger.

Each horse had been given ninety seconds to work each pen. The dark bay obviously had a good head on his shoulders, because he didn't spook at any of the obstacles. He cleared the log poles without a second glance, walked obediently around pylons and didn't so much as flinch at the bag of cans.

"Well, if I ever need to go on a trail ride, I won't have to worry about breaking my neck."

Wes had to agree. He liked the look in the animal's eyes, too. Even though they were high in the grandstand, he could tell the horse seemed calm and cool, as if nothing would faze him.

A horn sounded again. He sat up a little straighter.

"He's going to be great," he heard Jillian say.

Wes almost leaned forward and asked if she'd spoken to the horse personally. For some reason the thought amused him. Nobody could talk to animals, but wouldn't it be interesting if they could.

Once the gelding stepped into the middle ring, Wes knew they were in for a show. The rider stopped the gelding dead center, dropped the reins and waited for his horse to settle. Even so, Wes could see that the horse waited to be told to go. Like a rock in a slingshot, he wanted to shoot off. Sure enough, the moment the rider tapped the horse with a spur, the animal spun around his hind end so fast that his black mane seemed like streamers of liquid onyx. So fast that the animal appeared to sink low to the ground. So fast that his tail became wound up in his legs.

The audience roared.

"Impressive," Jillian said.

The rider stopped. Wes wondered if the tall, lanky cowboy on board the animal's back was dizzy. He sure would be. After a moment or two, he set off at a lope that was both beautiful to watch and clearly comfortable to ride. The horse's head was low, not too much but enough that Wes knew the animal respected the bit. He was in a snaffle, too, not one of those long-shanked implements of torture known as a spade bit. He watched as the horse changed directions, switched the leg he was leading with as effortlessly as a world-champion horse and continued on with his figure eight.

"I think I need to buy this horse," Natalie said.

"I think you'll be bidding against a lot of other people."

As if hearing him, the crowd erupted, this time at yet another flawless lead change. When the rider headed to the rail and began to pick up speed, everyone knew what came next. Wes held his breath as the animal headed toward the opposite end of the arena at a full-out run. If he'd blinked, he would have missed the cue the rider gave for the gelding to stop, which he did instantly, the horse seeming to sit down, back legs leaving twin skid marks in the dirt.

"Wow."

It was Jillian who'd spoken but the word was echoed by dozens around him.

"What is a horse like that doing at an auction like this?" Wes asked.

"That's a good question." Natalie shot him a glance. "I would expect him to be a futurity horse. He should be out earning money."

"He was raised on a cattle ranch," Jillian said. "The kid riding him is the owner's son. He learned about reining horses by watching YouTube videos."

Wes's mouth had dropped open. "He learned all that from a video?"

Jillian leaned forward, eyes twinkling. "Yup. And by studying the rulebook."

He clamped down on his lips just in time to stop a laugh. Unbelievable.

Whoever the kid was, he had a brilliant career ahead of him as a trainer. The gelding worked the rest of the pattern beautifully. When it came time to switch arenas, Wes expected to be disappointed with the way the animal handled cattle. He wasn't. He was half tempted to make a bid on the animal himself, except he strongly suspected the horse would sell for more money than he could afford.

"I hope jumping horses pays well."

Natalie didn't hesitate. "It does."

Of course it did. As with horse racing, the people involved had money, and lots of it. The purses for jumping competitions were pretty big, too. He'd heard Natalie had won a big grand prix not too long ago. It made sense that she had the means to afford a nice horse. Yeah, his buddy Colton Reynolds needed to meet her.

He'd probably appreciate meeting someone who wasn't a buckle bunny.

"You're not even watching the horse I picked out for you."

Huh? He turned toward the first arena and sure enough, there was the sorrel gelding with the four white socks. He looked tiny beneath the man who rode him, a big hulk of a cowboy with a bushy beard and black half chaps and spurs. Wes disliked him on sight.

You have to buy him.

Jillian's words reminded him that they did have something in common. They both hated animal abuse. He'd like to rake the man in the sides with his own spurs.

The little gelding barely glanced at the poles in the arena. He seemed unfazed by the bright orange pylons, too, and the audience watching him so intently. Jillian shot him a "See? I told you so" look. When the whistle sounded a little while later, he was curious to see how it would go. Like the man before him, the gelding's rider paused in the middle of the center arena. He no doubt planned to wow the crowd just as the last cowboy had done, only when he tapped the horse with his spur, the gelding erupted, and not in a good way.

The crowd gasped. Wes came half out of his seat as the demure sorrel gelding turned into the best-looking bronc he'd ever seen. One jump, two, three—the cowboy came off. Wes wouldn't have been human if he hadn't found himself amused. The man had it coming with the ice picks he used for spurs.

"Bad horsey." He could hear the laughter in Natalie's voice. He shot her a look that conveyed he agreed.

The horse had begun to run around. Much to his

credit, the gelding in the cutting arena—the big bay Natalie wanted to buy—hardly spared the little bronc a glance. His owner did, however, stopping the horse as officials ran for the man who lay in the arena. The cow the bay horse had been working ran up the rail nearest to the riderless horse, and Wes couldn't believe what happened next. The sorrel horse pinned its ears, snaked his head and tried to bite the little steer through the pipe-panel fence. Not only that, but he followed it along the rail. The cow, terrified, turned back in the other direction. So did the gelding. Back and forth the two of them worked, more than a few audience members laughing as the little animal doggedly stalked the calf.

"Too bad he'll be sifted," Natalie said.

He would, Wes agreed. Any animal caught misbehaving would be sent home. It was part of why the sale remained popular. You had a better-than-average chance of buying a good animal when all was said and done.

"I can't really blame the horse for bucking him off," he admitted.

"What do you mean?" Jillian's friend asked.

"That's the horse I was telling you about earlier," Jillian said. "The one with the spur marks on his sides."

Someone managed to intercept the animal on the rail, stopping the fun the gelding had been having with the steer. A few people in the crowd groaned. Wes wasn't the only one who'd been impressed by the gelding's natural ability.

"You're going to buy him."

The statement came from Jillian, and Wes couldn't believe his ears. "Excuse me?"

Jillian stood up, motioning to Natalie that they

should change places. His dog's tail thumped when he spotted his favorite human.

Traitor, he silently told the dog.

"He's going to be amazing, Wes." She sat down next to him. "I know he's not reining bred, but you saw him with that cow."

"He could be by Secretariat for all I care. He's a gelding. I can't breed him."

"He has ability. He would have cut that cow by himself if someone who knew what he was doing had been on his back."

Wes followed her gaze. The horse had been caught. Its head was down, sides heaving, tail swishing as it passed by its still-prone rider.

"I think he might have been hurt," Natalie observed.

No less than he deserved, but Wes kept the thought to himself. There was no excuse for leaving marks on a horse. If it misbehaved or behaved like a bronc, half the time the spurs had caused the problem, that or a bad-fitting saddle. Men like the guy in the arena—a man who would be okay, judging by the way he waved people away and slowly came to his feet—shouldn't be allowed to ride horses. They were bullies, pure and simple.

"What makes you think that horse doesn't have some serious mental issues?"

But he didn't need to wait for her answer, and he almost shook his head.

"I just know," she said.

His gaze shot to her own. She had a way of looking at him. A challenge shone from her eyes, but there was also a plea, one that begged him to trust her.

Son of a—

"All right." He couldn't keep himself from shaking his head this time, though. "I'll take a look. But you know he's going to be sifted. I won't be able to buy him at the auction. It'd have to be a private treaty sale."

"All the better. After what just happened, they'll all but give him away. You could probably buy him out behind the barn right now."

"For good reason."

She placed a hand on his thigh. His gaze quickly moved to where her fingers rested, Wes wanting to move his leg out of the way, stopping himself just in time, wondering why he minded her touch so much.

"Just give him a shot."

Her hand, those eyes… He had to look away. "Okay, fine."

But he got up before he changed his mind. No, before he convinced himself he should give something else a try…like touching her back, maybe even kissing the woman with the kind green eyes.

Chapter Five

She didn't have a hard time finding the owner of the sorrel. All she had to do was go out behind the barns, where, just as she expected, the man had the gelding at the end of a lead rope, lunge whip in his hand.

"Don't you *dare* hit him!"

The jerk masquerading as a cowboy flew around to face her. She wanted to run forward and grab the whip from his hand.

It's okay, she told the horse.

The animal stood there, head thrown up in terror, nostrils flaring, feet braced as if waiting for the next blow…which he was.

"Get the hell out of here."

"I want to buy that horse." The declaration had popped out of her mouth before she could stop them. If Wes wouldn't get this horse away from his owner, she would, although she had no idea how she'd afford the purchase price, much less the cost to transport him home.

The cowboy tugged the brim of his hat down low, eyes as dark as the irises of a snake's. He'd taken off his half chaps, but he still wore his jeans and white button-down, although that shirt was stained by arena mud.

He had body-builder shoulders and with his black beard and dark eyes he reminded her of Bluto, a cartoon bully from a decades-old television show.

"You can't buy him." The man's hand lowered. The tip of the long whip touched the ground. "He's been booted from the sale."

"Doesn't mean I can't buy him." Sensing the man's obstinacy, she quickly added, "But if you don't want to sell him today, that's okay."

She forced herself to turn away, told her feet to take steps even though every fiber of her being cried out to stand her ground. That horse…that poor horse. She had to save him.

"How much you willing to pay?" the cowboy called out.

"I want to try him first."

Jillian's whole body reacted to the words, an involuntary jolt that had her whirling around to face Wes. She hadn't even seen him follow her, but there he stood, with Cowboy sitting at his feet, panting, tongue out—as if they'd both run to catch up to her.

"Who are you?" Bluto asked.

Wes's gaze found her own. She smiled, so happy to see him she wanted to run over and hug him.

"I'm Wes Landon, not that it matters. The point is I want to buy your horse."

They both turned to face the man who still held the reins of the horse. The poor animal hadn't relaxed one iota. His sorrel coat had started to darken from sweat.

You have *to buy him.*

She realized she'd looked up and spoken to Wes with her eyes. She'd felt him staring at her. Strangely, though, he seemed to understand.

"Let me get on him." But he spoke to her, not the man.

"Did you see what happened in there?" Bluto asked.

"I sure did."

"And you still want to try him?"

"The sooner, the better."

A breath she hadn't even known she'd been holding breezed past her lips. She had no need for a cutting horse, but she'd have taken this one home even if it'd meant riding him back and begging people for a second job.

"There's no cattle to work him on," the man said.

"That's okay. I can work him without a cow. I mainly want to see if I can stay on."

"Yeah, good luck with that."

Wes headed toward the horse, but he leaned toward her and said, "It's funny how you warn me away from one horse, yet insist I ride an animal that just bucked a man off."

"It's not the horse's fault."

The man turned back to the horse when they reached him, but the reaction of the sorrel was immediate, scooting backward so fast he almost jerked the reins from the man's hands."

"Knock it off, you son of a—"

"Here." Wes jumped forward and slipped between man and horse. "Let me take those." He didn't wait for the owner to respond, just took the two reins and blocked the man from approaching the gelding. "What's his name?"

With a glance in her direction, one that conveyed the ominous portent of a thundercloud, Bluto said, "Dudley."

Jillian stepped forward. "His registered name is Dudley Dual Right."

She loved the name. Honestly, she'd spotted it in the program and known she'd had to see him. Sometimes that happened, too…a feeling. She'd had one about this young colt.

Hopefully he won't break Wes's neck.

"Hey there, bud," she heard Wes say softly, so softly the horse's ears flicked forward and back as if straining to listen. "It's okay, son. I'm not going to hurt you."

"Son of a bitch deserved to be whipped."

And maybe we should beat the crud out of you for being such a poor rider.

The words were on the tip of Jillian's tongue, but she didn't dare say them out loud, not when she wanted so badly to buy the horse. That was her plan. If Wes didn't take the gelding, she would. Natalie would help her purchase him and know what to do with him.

"Come on." Wes gave the reins a gentle tug. The gelding resisted for a moment, but when he realized Wes wasn't going to jerk on his mouth or hit him, he obediently followed, Cowboy trailing at their heels.

It's okay.

The horse's ears flicked again, and Jillian knew he'd heard her. His head even dropped, not that Wes would notice. Not that he'd believe her even if she pointed it out. Men were just that way.

The activity in the barn area increased the closer they moved toward the main facility. Horses trotted. People called out to one another. Grooms worked to get the best shine on a horse's coat. She noticed that Wes kept his attention on the animal by his side. He absently stroked a piece of copper-colored mane as he murmured quietly to the gelding. Dual Rey, one of cutting's all-time leading sires, had been a redhead, too. She had to admit he had sure been trying to cut that cow like Dual Rey. Couldn't Wes see that? He was a good colt in the wrong hands. By the time they got to the arena, the animal clearly understood Wes wasn't going to flog him.

"Name's Gordon."

Jillian hardly looked at the man; she was too focused on projecting mental images to Dudley of Wes getting on his back. Of a good ride. Of green pastures and warm stalls. Of the life he would have once they bought him.

"Okay, here goes."

They stood by the entrance of the arena. Cowboy glanced around, spotted her, then came to sit by her feet. Jillian found herself squatting down and stroking the dog's head while she waited for Wes to mount. He was busy tugging on the girth to make sure it wasn't loose. Next he checked the length of the stirrups and then glanced at the bridle. After one last pat, he positioned himself to mount.

Jillian's breath held.

She knew the animal wasn't bad. Knew he wasn't the type to intentionally hurt a human. Still. Horses could be like children. Unpredictable.

Wes swung a leg over the horse's back. Nothing happened. He settled his hat more firmly on his head before standing in the stirrups and shifting from side to side, the girth apparently tight enough to suit his needs, because he gently sat back down again. Still, the horse didn't move.

"Can you open the gate?"

She wasn't sure if he spoke to her or Gordon, but Jillian rushed forward to do as asked. Dudley moved forward when Wes lightly tapped his sides. The whole time he spoke softly to the animal, patting his neck.

It was crowded inside the practice arena. Jillian had to lift her hand to shield her eyes from the sun. Dust clouded the air. Spurs clinked. The slobber chains attached to the horses' bits jangled. In the distance a horse neighed. The metal rail was cold beneath Jillian's hand as she leaned against it. She admired the way Wes sat on a horse. He didn't choke up on the reins, something the horse seemed to appreciate. Dudley's head dropped, his long mane dangling down his neck. He was a young horse—all harsh angles and big head—but one day he would fill out, and Jillian just knew he'd be stunning.

She saw Wes pick up the reins. The gelding instantly tensed, as if he expected a sharp stab of the spurs and a flick of the reins, but Wes merely clucked and squeezed with his whole leg, not with the rowels of his spurs. The animal obediently moved into a trot. Beside her, she felt more than saw the man relax. He'd obviously been expecting a bronc.

"He's going to be a good one," Gordon said.

She had no doubt, but not with Gordon on his back. Wes had just proved himself ten times the rider the horse's owner was. He had a relaxed way of sitting in the saddle. Jillian had watched enough show jumping over the years to appreciate the way he pressed his heels down in the stirrups. So many Western riders rode flat-footed, legs kicked out in front of them. They didn't utilize the center of gravity crucial to expert horsemanship. Wes did. Not only that, but his hands were light with the reins. He spoke to the animal, too, and the sight of his lips moving, the way he patted the animal when he obediently moved into a slow lope, the soft way he sat in the saddle—it all made her smile like a fool. He could ride. Well.

Why did that matter?

She refused to examine the question. Instead, she watched as Wes reversed direction. The longer he rode, the more Dudley relaxed. When Wes pulled the horse to a stop on the other side of the rail, he had a small smile on his face.

"You like him?" Gordon wore a salesman's grin. "You should. He's got the bloodlines and the talent to make a name for himself. Reining. Cutting. He's bred to do it all."

"If you don't get dumped on your keister on a regular basis."

The man's jowls turned red. "That was just a fluke."

"Something tells me otherwise, but I still want to see one more thing before I agree to buy him."

Jillian's heart leaped. He wasn't going to let the horse go back to that awful man. Thank the Lord.

"What's that?" Gordon glanced between the two of them. "I'm not willing to let him go on a trial, if that's what you're thinking."

"That's not it at all." Wes whistled. Cowboy bolted toward his master. "I just want to ride him out back for a bit."

Jillian could tell that the man didn't like the idea. He probably figured Wes hadn't been bucked off in the arena, but it was a good bet he might be outside of it. She wondered what was going on, too, but she opened the gate nonetheless. Cowboy fell into step beside his master. They headed toward the back of the fairgrounds. The three of them—well, five if one counted Cowboy and Dudley—all walking down a dusty road like compadres at the OK Corral. Around them hundreds of vehicles, most of them trucks, sat parked, half of them pulling horse trailers. Wes took them to a spot far out back, to a large grass field used by the herding-dog people. They held an annual competition the same weekend as the bull-and-gelding sale but it stood empty now.

"Cowboy, go!"

The dog immediately brightened at Wes's command. He charged toward the pasture as if looking for stray cows. Clearly, that was what Wes wanted, although Jillian still had no idea what Wes was up to.

"Cowboy, down." The dog hit the ground so hard the movement resembled a canine belly flop.

"Damn." Gordon crossed his arms and glanced up at Wes. "That's a well-trained dog."

"You have no idea," Wes said, walking into the field and approaching the dog. Jillian knew then what Wes intended to do, although it was mostly the way Cowboy eyed his master that helped her figure it out. The dog stared at Wes and his horse as if a side of beef hung off it.

"Get him," Wes ordered the dog.

Cowboy lunged, then stopped a few feet in front of the horse, squatting on his front legs and barking as if asking the animal to play. Wes just sat there, but the horse dropped his head and when Cowboy darted right, Wes leaned the reins against the horse's neck, a silent cue that he should follow the dog. Dudley needed no prompting. It was the funniest thing Jillian had ever seen. Horse and dog faced off against each other, Cowboy's tail wagging as the horse mirrored his moves. Left. Right. Left again. Cowboy took off at one point, running a few dozen feet, Dudley doing the same thing. When Cowboy stopped, so did the horse.

"I'll be damned."

Jillian silently echoed Gordon's sentiment. Dog and horse played a game of cat and mouse, the horse moving so quickly at times that he left deep furrows in the grass. Cowboy loved it. If canines had grins, his was from cheek to cheek. Dudley did, too. There was no doubt the horse had talent. After his display in the arena trailing the steer up the rail and now this, Jillian knew Wes would be a fool not to buy the horse and at least give him a chance.

"Whoa," he said softly.

The animal promptly obeyed.

Good boy, she silently told the horse.

"What do you think?" Gordon said.

"Not bad," Wes replied. "Not bad at all."

Jillian couldn't keep the smile from slipping onto her face.

Not bad.

That was an understatement. He knew it and she knew it. The horse might just be pure gold.

Chapter Six

Wes tried not to show his excitement. It wouldn't do for Gordon to catch on to how badly he wanted to buy his horse.

Unbelievable.

That was how it'd felt being on Dudley's back. It was as if they'd connected. A perfect pair. His yin to the horse's yang. Magic.

But Gordon didn't need to know that. Far from it. So he slipped off the horse's back, gave him a pat and headed back to the barn. Something jerked him back. Dudley. The horse had grabbed his shirt.

"Hey."

Dudley's ears were pricked forward, mischief in his eyes. He even tossed his head as if silently saying, "What you gonna do about that?"

"He likes you."

Wes just nodded, afraid to look into Jillian's eyes. Afraid she'd see his thoughts somehow, which sounded insane because it wasn't as though she could read minds. It just seemed that way.

"So do you want him?"

The question came from Gordon, but Wes just shrugged. He wanted him, all right, but the first rule of negotiation was to appear indifferent about the item you wanted to purchase.

"I'll give you a really good deal."

Now they were talking. Wes had to bite back a smile. "How good?"

They were walking between the parked cars and trucks, Dudley following meekly behind. The horse didn't appear bothered by the vehicles searching for a parking space or the people walking to and from cars or the loose dogs that always seemed to accompany equestrian events. In the distance he could hear the sound of the announcer calling exhibitor numbers to people outside the arena waiting for their chance to work.

"I have to have at least five."

Thousand? The man was off his rocker.

"Not going to pay that much."

Wes glanced up at the sky, pretending an interest in the weather.

"Okay, so why don't you make me an offer."

He didn't answer right away. Let the man sweat it. After the way he'd treated Dudley, he deserved it.

He walked all the way back to the barn area, then paused near the arena to say, "Where's your stall?"

Wes knew perfectly well where it was, but he didn't let Gordon in on the secret. He glanced at Jillian. She seemed amused. He knew in that moment that she understood the game he played.

"It's over there. On the other side of the row of stalls there."

The man pointed with his chin to an area with walnut trees. Wes headed in that direction.

"Look, I'm not going to accept less than three for

him. He's got the bloodlines to be successful at a lot of things."

Wes stopped. Cowboy dropped to his haunches at his feet. "A winning sire doesn't mean a hill of beans, especially since he's a gelding, and especially since I won't be using him for what he's bred to do—reining."

Gordon had begun to look more and more disconcerted. Wes waited until he was almost back to the man's stall before saying, "I'll give you twenty-two for him."

"Done."

The way the man leaped at the offer, Wes wondered how many times good old Gordon had been dumped on his rear. And maybe he'd made a mistake, but at least he wouldn't be into the gelding for much.

"You won't regret this."

Oddly, Wes thought he might be right. "Why don't you untack him? I'll head back to my truck and get the money."

"Sure. No problem."

The man reached for the reins. Dudley backed away so fast it was all Wes could do to hold on to the reins. "Whoa there, boy," he told the horse. Wes was certain the poor animal had been abused. "It's okay."

You won't ever be struck again, he silently told the horse. He gently touched the animal and was rewarded by a dropped head and a softening of the animal's eyes. When Gordon came up behind him, he slowly handed off the reins.

I'll be right back, he assured the horse.

Jillian and Cowboy both fell into step alongside him. She didn't say anything but once again he found himself reading her expression with ease. The woman was the classified section of a newspaper.

"Well?" she finally said when they were out of earshot. "What did you think?"

"I think he's got great potential."

She came off the ground, pumped the air with a fist, let out a woot. Cowboy took a few startled steps back. "I knew it!"

"Stupid son of a cuss doesn't know what he has."

"That's because he's a stupid son of a cuss. I know for a fact that the cinch was pinching him today. That's why he bucked."

"And how do you know that?"

She opened her mouth, then closed it again. He had a feeling she'd been about to say something but had fished it back just in time. "I could just tell."

"Really."

She nodded, black bob flicking forward. "Let's face it. Gordon there isn't exactly model thin." She made a sound, something between a snort and a guffaw that reminded him of a seal barking. It nearly stopped him in his tracks. "Can you imagine having him on your back?"

"That's not a visual I want to imagine."

She made that sound again, and Wes found himself admitting he found it strangely adorable.

"But I guess it doesn't matter." He met her gaze. "Something drew you to that horse, and I'm glad it did. Bad or good today, I would have bought him even if he'd bucked me off. There was no way I was going to let that idiot touch him ever again."

She didn't say anything. Wes suddenly felt like a bug under a microscope. Her green eyes studied his own, and not just his eyes. Her gaze darted over his face, his lips, his nose, his eyes—all of it was scanned, as if she sought an answer she didn't expect to find.

"You really love horses, don't you?"

"I do." He glanced toward the arena, where horses were still being worked. "And I have a lot riding on this one."

There she went studying him like a raven again. It made him realize he probably should have kept that to himself. She didn't need to know about the codicil to his father's will, the one that had been in his father's father's will…and his great-grandfather's will. The codicil that had ensured the Landons' wealth for over a century. The bulk of his family's fortune could not be inherited unless he proved himself first. He needed to make his own fortune, and he had until he was twenty-eight to do so.

"You don't act like someone raised with a silver spoon, either."

The observation was so astute and so close to the mark that Wes turned back toward the barn.

"I better get back to Gordon before he thinks I changed my mind." He looked down at his dog. "Come on, Cowboy."

"Wait."

He swung back to face her.

"Are you going to stick around for the auction tomorrow night?"

"No." He shook his head. "Not now that I've found a horse."

To his surprise, she seemed disappointed. "Then I guess this is goodbye."

He stuffed his hands in his pockets. He had to. He had the strangest urge to hug her. "For now."

"Wes, you don't really have to help CEASE. It was a joke. I was trying to get your goat."

"No." He smiled. "I want to help."

He wanted to see her again. The realization had him rocking back on his toes.

So what if she's a little different? He could deal with that. Look at how he'd dealt with Maxine. Then again, maybe Maxine wasn't a good comparison. There was crazy...and then there was *muy loco.*

Too late to take the offer back, though. Hope had bloomed in her eyes like a summer sunflower, and so had relief, and the craziest thing of all, what made him look away in dismay, was how she made him want to promise other things. Like moonlit rides and romantic dinners on a beach.

"Then I guess this isn't goodbye."

When their gazes connected, Wes saw her smile. The gentleness of her soul made her green eyes glow brighter. He'd noticed her looks yesterday, but the purity of her goodness outshone the beauty of her smile.

"I'll call you when I get back to town."

He walked away before he could have any other bizarre thoughts. Like how good she smelled—vanilla and berries—and how the combination of the sweetness in her eyes and her sugary smell made him want to do something completely irrational, like kiss her.

HOW LONG SHE stood there, watching as Wes headed toward his trailer, Jillian didn't know.

Goodbye, Cowboy.

The dog paused by his master's side, turned back for a second, brown eyes blinking. She'd learned a long time ago that canines said goodbye that way—with a long blink. Cats did the same thing but for a different reason. It was a sign of love and affection, but you had to stare at them for a moment or two to spot it.

Of course, Wes would never believe her, and therein lay the crux of the problem, because she'd started to like Wes a little too much. The man had a hard time believing she had a good eye for picking out horses. What would he say if she told him she could talk to animals? He might humor her at first, but deep down inside, he'd call her crazy.

Stupid. Haven't you learned your lesson already? Relationships are always doomed to fail, especially with men who don't believe in your abilities.

With a sigh of regret she turned away. Natalie was right: maybe she should learn to keep her emotions out of the mix and simply use men for sex. She knew plenty of women who operated that way. She just didn't think she could ever be one of them.

"You ready to get some dinner?" she asked her friend once she found her in the grandstands.

Natalie was all smiles. "You missed that dark gray colt we were interested in. He was fantastic. Think I want him, too. But yeah, sure, let's go eat, although if it's just the same to you, I'd rather not have any more greasy fries and hamburgers." Natalie patted her flat belly.

Jillian glanced toward the arena, where another three horses worked. "We can drive somewhere."

"Cool." Natalie bounded up from her seat. "But I get to choose where we go." Her friend's gaze slid past Jillian. "Where's Wes?"

Jillian shrugged. "He just bought a horse."

Natalie's blue eyes opened wide, her long blond lashes nearly touching her eyebrows. "Really?"

As they made their way toward Natalie's truck, Jillian filled her in on the details. Her friend couldn't believe they'd found Dudley being beaten behind the barn, but once Jillian explained the spur marks, she nodded in agreement that Wes had been a hero for buying the gelding.

"He seems nice." They reached her red truck—aka Lola—the unlock button giving a chirp as her friend pressed it. "Good thing you came along when you did."

Natalie made a nice living jumping horses, and nothing demonstrated that better than the brand-new truck she drove. She made an even nicer living training people to jump their own horses.

"Did any of the other horses we liked perform well?" Jillian asked as she slid into the passenger seat.

"Yeah, actually. But I think I like that dark bay horse best of all." She turned the key.

The truck coughed. They both looked toward the hood in chagrin.

"That didn't sound good." Natalie tried it again. This time it didn't so much cough as sputter, the truck emitting a dying gasp.

"Oh, crap."

"It's brand-new." Jillian glanced around at the other trucks parked nearby, although why she did that she had no idea. It wasn't as if a repairman would be standing there with a wrench in hand waiting to rescue two damsels in distress. "Is it out of diesel?"

"We filled it up the day we arrived, remember?" Natalie tried it one more time. The whole truck shuddered.

"I think it's broken."

"You think?" Natalie hit the steering wheel with her hands. "Now what? I don't know diddly doo-doo about trucks."

"Better call AAA."

But it would be at least an hour before someone could come out and tow the truck. Meanwhile, they opened the hood—as if they'd have a snowball's chance in hell of diagnosing what was wrong.

"Maybe it's a loose wire or something?" Jillian said.

They both peered into the engine compartment.

"Need some help?"

Wes.

Crazy that she recognized his voice instantly. Crazier still that her heart leaped when she heard it. Despite telling herself a million times to maintain her distance, she couldn't keep a welcoming smile off her face.

And that was the craziest thing of all.

Chapter Seven

DOA.

Jillian could tell by the look on Wes's face when he emerged from beneath her friend's truck. He reached for his black cowboy hat and shoved it back on.

"Oh, crap," Natalie said, apparently reading Wes's expression, too.

"You're not going to believe this." He wiped his hands on a rag Jillian had found in her trailer. "Someone stole your catalytic converter."

"My *what*?"

Jillian knew what it was. "No way."

Wes tossed the rag onto the hood of the truck. "It happens. They steal them for the precious metals, like platinum and rhodium. Looks like you got hit while you were inside. Have you driven it at all since you got here?"

"No. I have my trailer." Natalie pointed to the long white horse trailer with living quarters in the front, which was parked behind her truck.

"Then it could have been last night, too, while you were sleeping."

"Son of a—" Natalie bit off the end of her curse, but Jillian could tell she wanted to let it fly.

"Do you have insurance?" Wes asked.

"Of course," Natalie answered.

"Good, 'cause these things cost a bundle. And depending on the local dealership, you might be here awhile. They don't exactly keep catalytic converters in stock."

"You sound like you've heard of this happening before," Jillian said.

"I have. I was at a competition last year where a bunch of trucks got hit. It happens at horse shows, too. Crooks aren't as stupid as people think."

Natalie turned to her. "How will we get home?"

"We won't." Jillian gave her a reassuring smile. "Not until it's fixed."

"But the Taylors want you to go look at that horse on Sunday. That's a big deal, with the potential for more clients if you play your cards right."

"That's three days from now. Besides, I can reschedule if push comes to shove."

"They might not like that. You know how wealthy people are sometimes."

"She can go home with me."

The words had the effect of a stick of dynamite. Both Natalie and Jillian stared at Wes. Natalie was the first to look away, but only to shoot Jillian a wink of amusement, one that clearly projected, *He wants to take you home with him.*

She ignored her and met Wes's gaze again. "You don't have to do that."

"It's a great idea." Natalie took a step forward. "My barn is closed on Monday and with any luck they'll have the part in by then. I can drive home with my new horse, if I end up buying one tomorrow night, I mean."

"The only problem is, I'm leaving tonight."

Tonight.

"Actually, just as soon as I load up Dudley. It's at least a seven-hour drive back home and I'd like to try and make it back by midnight."

"You'd be home tomorrow." Natalie nodded, as if she had the power to make the decision for her. "You wouldn't have to reschedule the Taylors."

"I'm sure they would understand—"

"You know how hard it is to rearrange things when more than one person is involved, not to mention the impression you might give them."

"But I'll miss the sale."

"I call you with the details."

"No, I—"

Don't want to be alone with Wes.

She didn't want to risk spending more time with him. Didn't want to find out that he had yet another wonderful quality, one that would make it even harder to keep her distance.

Damn it.

"I don't need a ride, but thanks." She forced herself to smile.

"Not a problem." Wes fished his cell phone out of his pocket. "Let's call the dealership."

But it was worse than he'd predicted. Two days, minimum, to get the part. And they weren't the only ones hit that night, either. Seemed a bunch of people had lost their catalytic converters. Monday might have been an optimistic guess with so many parts on order. The dealership told them it could be four or five days.

"You're going home with Wes," Natalie pronounced.

Jillian knew her friend was right. She didn't have an

assistant trainer as Natalie did, someone who could pick up the slack in her absence. She had a busy day scheduled for Tuesday. Another new customer and a few of her regular ones, too. She would lose out on hundreds of dollars if she didn't get back soon.

"Well?" Wes asked.

Jillian glanced at Wes, her spirits sinking. "Okay, I'll go."

THEY LEFT AS soon as he loaded up Dudley, and Wes was glad to note the colt climbed in the trailer easily. It was dark outside by the time they were ready to head out, Wes having waited around for the tow truck to arrive. Fortunately, Natalie had living quarters in her horse trailer. She'd be stuck at the show grounds for the next few days, but she didn't seem to mind. Lots of cute cowboys, she'd said. Plenty to keep her occupied.

The latch on the door of the new three-horse trailer soundlessly closed. He'd scrimped and saved for years before he'd been able to afford it, but as he'd told his mom, it'd been an investment in his future. He hoped the horse inside turned out to be a good investment, too.

"Come on, Cowboy. Let's go home."

Jillian had already taken a seat inside the truck. She turned to look at him when he opened the driver's-side door, Cowboy jumping into the crew cab first. The dog settled in the back, but he obviously hadn't noticed Jillian inside the truck at first, because suddenly he paused, and his black tail began to wag when he noticed their guest.

"Hey there, Cowboy," Jillian said softly.

Wes slid in next. He could barely see Jillian or his dog until he started the vehicle and the lights from the dash cast a martianlike glow over the cab. The tense lines on her brow had him alert.

"You okay?"

"Fine."

That didn't sound promising. "You could always go camp out in the living quarters."

"While we're driving?"

"Why not?"

"Isn't that illegal?"

"I promise not to tell anyone."

She leaned back. "That's okay. I'll take my chances in here."

He started the truck, mulling over that phrase in his head. *Take my chances.* What did *that* mean?

"You can sleep if you want. I promise not to disturb you."

"Not sleepy."

"Hungry? I have snacks."

"I grabbed a bite while waiting for the tow truck."

What was wrong with her? She'd been so warm and friendly earlier. He'd thought she'd be excited to help bring Dudley home, had even hoped to discuss his plans for the colt. Instead, she sat next to him like a frog on a log.

He concentrated on navigating the crowded parking area for a moment and then the road, searching for something to say. It would be a long ride if all they did was sit in silence.

"What made you want to become a trainer?"

She glanced at him quickly, almost as if the question took her by surprise. "I really didn't have a choice. It sort of picked me."

"Oh, yeah? How's that?"

She shifted in her seat, looking uncomfortable about the question. "It's a long story."

"We have seven hours."

"You won't believe me."

"Believe what?"

When he looked over at her, she appeared to be pondering what he'd said. As he turned his head to focus back on the road, he caught a whiff of her unique scent—vanilla and berries. He'd smelled it earlier and the damn thing had stayed with him all afternoon, and he'd wondered more than once if she tasted as good as she smelled—like a damn cobbler.

"It happened when I was fifteen."

He could spare only a quick glance. He'd made the light and so they were merging onto the freeway now. Fortunately, traffic was sparse.

"Right after I lost my mom."

Her mom had died? He glanced at her in time to spot the sadness on her face.

"There'd always been…issues with Mom. My dad left us both when I was younger. I never really noticed his absence. My mom just seemed to make it work, but she'd always been prone to bouts of depression."

It seemed she got lost in memories for a moment, because she became quiet. He didn't want to push her, just kept his eyes on the narrow white line, respecting her privacy.

"I should have known something was wrong when she didn't pick me up from my riding lesson, but I just figured she'd forgotten, caught a ride with someone else. I had no idea what was coming. When you're young, you never think about death. Tally, our golden retriever, was at the door, and he greeted me as he always did, all goofy dog smiles and wagging tail, and I was in such a hurry to take a shower that I headed to the bathroom without even wondering where she was, only when I opened the door…"

She didn't need to spell it out. He had the strangest urge to lay a hand over her own.

"I thought at first she'd just fallen. You know, she was lying there, but she didn't move when I called her name and that's when I knew." She shook her head. "I don't remember much about what happened next. I just remember Tally shoving her head against mine. I must have called 911 but still don't remember doing it. I just kept thinking, 'What happened? What happened?'" She turned to look at him. "And then somehow I just knew."

He took a deep breath. "Knew what?"

"My mom hit her head in the bedroom."

"But you said she was in the bathroom."

"I know, but I just knew what had happened to her. It freaked me out, but the paramedics arrived and they were taking my mom." Another head shake. From the backseat Cowboy whined. "I forgot about it until the medical examiner called my aunt with the cause of death. Blunt-force trauma to the head. They later found blood, actually a trail of it leading from the dresser in her room to where I'd found her."

Okay, so the story gave him chills. "Maybe you saw that blood. Maybe that's how you knew."

"The spots were microscopic. There was no way I knew."

So what was she saying? That she was psychic?

"I had to go live with my aunt. Like I said, my dad took off and he didn't want a thing to do with me, so Tally and I moved to my aunt Linda's ranch. Best thing that could have happened to me. Months later one of her horses cut its leg. We didn't know how, but I somehow knew exactly where he'd injured himself. We found evidence later. Freaked my aunt out. That's another story. Thank goodness Aunt Linda is open-minded or she might have put me in a loony bin."

She *was* claiming to be psychic.

What was it with him? Did he attract crazy people? First Maxine and now Jillian.

Except…

She didn't seem crazy. *What if…?*

No, he quickly told himself. She was just really good at reading animal body language. That was all.

But the head injury…

He still refused to believe it. It was all just too… bizarre.

"So you went to live with your aunt." He needed to change the subject. "But it all worked out."

She shrugged. "It was tough at first." She turned to stare out the window. They'd left town, an inky blackness the only thing outside the car's cabin. They were in one of those rare pockets of space where nobody rode behind them or in front, and no homes or buildings or industrial areas were around, just open land with a few distant homes dotting the landscape. Traffic in the other direction seemed nonexistent, too. Just the two of them in the cab of the truck—well, and Cowboy and Dudley in the back.

As if sensing his thoughts, his dog whined again. He absently reached out and patted Cowboy's head.

"It couldn't have been easy to lose your mom right when you needed her most. Teenage years. No fun."

She nodded. "I don't think I would have survived if

Aunt Linda hadn't owned a ranch. It wasn't until college that I decided to train horses full-time, but I majored in animal science just in case. I about lost my mind being away from my four-legged friends."

You mean you hadn't lost it before?

It wouldn't have been a nice thing to say. He knew that, but it went to show how hard it was for him to accept that she had any kind of psychic abilities.

"Must play hell on your love life."

The comment had slipped out, Wes not thinking straight after her whole "I know things" speech, but she turned toward him so fast he knew he'd struck a nerve.

"What makes you say that?"

Wait. They'd been talking about horse training, not her psychic abilities. "I just meant people can be such skeptics."

Hypocrite. You're a skeptic.

"Yeah, but as it turns out, that's the least of my problems."

The last part had been barely audible over the sound of the truck's engines, but he heard it nonetheless.

"What problems?"

"Nothing," she said quickly.

But he turned to her right as a vehicle's headlights caught her eyes, just in time for him to glimpse the emotions within them. Pain. Sadness. Maybe even longing.

"We all have skeletons in our closet." He had a big one, too, although his was related to family.

"Yeah, but there are skeletons, and then there's a big old Tyrannosaurus rex."

That didn't sound good. None of it sounded good. She'd just admitted she thought she had some kind of psychic ability. On the heels of that she'd admitted to having another, bigger problem. There should have been a big sign hanging over her head flashing Warning, Warning, Warning. Crazy Woman.

Except she didn't seem crazy. And he couldn't forget the sadness he'd seen in her eyes. And she'd just demonstrated that her gut feelings were pretty spot-on, so maybe she wasn't crazy after all.

And why are you making excuses for her?

Because he liked her, damn it. He liked her a lot. He just didn't know what to do about it.

Chapter Eight

As a conversation killer, her words had done the trick. Jillian had been kicking herself ever since.

Why had she made herself sound like such a crackpot? She should never have admitted that sometimes she just knew things. The look on his face…

She bit back a sigh of disappointment.

It had said it all. If he reacted that way to that little bit of news, what would he say if she told him the truth—that she saw pictures in her mind? Pictures that animals gave to her. That in a strange way she could talk to animals. He'd call her a wackadoodle for sure.

They'd spent the better part of the next hour in near silence, Wes seemingly content to leave her to her thoughts, her stupid ridiculous thoughts featuring a man like Wes at the center of them. Well, a man like Wes who didn't think she was crazy. She peeked at him. He fit the bill in every other way, though. Too bad he'd never be anything more to her than a friend.

When they reached Sacramento, they spoke again, but only to discuss whether she wanted to stop and stretch her legs. She shook her head. All she wanted to do was get home. Wes had agreed to drop her at her house on his way through Via Del Caballo. The ranch where he lived was on the coast, over the hill from the main part of town, but her place was right on his route home and so he'd insisted he didn't mind.

"Why don't you get some sleep?" he said an hour outside Sacramento. "We still have a long ways to go."

"That's okay. I have a hard time sleeping when someone else is driving."

He shot her a smile. "Don't trust me?"

She liked his smile. "I don't think it's fair."

What he'd been about to say was interrupted by the sound of his cell phone. He pressed the hands-free button on his steering wheel once he recognized the number on his dashboard's display. "Hey, Mom."

"You on your way?" He glanced at Jillian and offered a silent apology.

"I am. Be home around midnight."

"Not any sooner?"

The question had him glancing at her again, an expression of surprise on his face. "Why? Is there something wrong?"

"We have a bit of a situation."

His hands tightened on the steering wheel. "What is it? What's wrong?"

"Nothing bad. Calm down. You just need to get home as soon as possible."

"Mom. I'm hauling a horse. If I drive any faster, I'll risk a wreck."

"I know that. Of course I know that. I'm just suggesting you keep the pit stops to a minimum."

Her stomach flipped over.

"You can't just make a request like that without an explanation. I'll be worried sick the whole way home."

"Like I said, it's nothing life threatening, honey. Life altering, yes, but that's all."

"Life altering?"

"See you when you get here."

"Mom—"

They both heard her sigh. "Wesley Landon, I'm not going to say it again. Everything's fine here at the ranch, but something's come up that needs your immediate attention. I just need you to get here as quickly as possible…that's all."

Clearly, he knew his mom well enough to know when to stop pushing her, because Jillian watched him shake his head in frustration. "Fine. I'll get there as quickly as I can."

She hung up.

"Damn it."

"Do you want me to drive?"

"No. I'm just frustrated. I hate it when she gets all cryptic like that. Let me just call one of our ranch hands, though, just to make sure everything's okay."

But Jorge assured him all was well. If there was a problem, it had to be something else and Jillian could tell it worried him.

"Let me know if you need a break. And don't worry about stopping. I have the bladder of an elephant."

He looked at her, amusement flickering on his face. "Good to know."

But the drive seemed interminable to them both. Jillian tried to distract him with some of her more amusing animal stories. Funny how the tension in the truck had completely shifted away from her and to Wes. Frankly, she was happy it had. She didn't need any more questions from him.

"How far off the freeway do you live?"

"Don't worry about me," she said, waving him forward. "Just get home. I can have Mariah pick me up."

"No, I'll drive you."

She shook her head. "It will take an extra half hour at the very least to drop me off. Besides, I already texted her and she agreed to come get me."

That seemed to settle the matter. Even so, it was just after midnight when they pulled up to a horse farm she'd spotted at least a hundred times on her way up the coast. Only now did she put two and two together. Twin granite pillars held iron cutouts forming initials— L.F.—done in an elegant scroll that she now knew stood for *Landon Farms*.

"This is your mom's place?"

They had crossed over low-lying hills. Off in the distance she could just make out the metallic glow of the ocean. There was no full moon overhead, but she didn't need to see it to know what lay beyond. She had memorized every detail of the coastal horse farm the many times she'd passed by. Between smaller granite pillars that mimicked the ones at the entrance brown fence boards stretched for what seemed like miles. Grass that always looked perfectly clipped, whether by horses' teeth or a slew of gardeners, reminded Jillian of Kentucky. This close to the ocean, coastal rains kept everything green. The farm had been built back from the road a ways. It was shielded from view by the swell of the land. She knew that from farther down the highway a person could catch sight of the massive white stables, one with a dark green gable roof and a tall spire in the middle. She'd always assumed the farm raised Thoroughbreds. Now that she knew better, Jillian was find-

ing it somewhat strange to be passing through the gates
of a place she'd admired for so long from a distance.

"You okay?" She'd asked the question because a
quick look at Wes's face revealed he was far, far away.
Lines of tension bracketed his mouth and eyes.

"I just wish I knew what was going on."

"You'll know in a moment."

They crossed through the gates, following a black-
top road that seemed to disappear between the swell of
two small hills. The land sloped downward, toward the
ocean in the distance, the curve of the hills blocking
their view of the ranch house. But not for long. Once
they passed between them, a small valley opened up,
and there it was on her right, the stable she'd been able
to glimpse from the highway. It was gilded by moon-
light, but even if it had been a cloudy night, it would
have been hard to miss. Across from it, separated by a
massive circular driveway the size of a football field,
was the main house—definitely *not* a farmhouse—the
home a granite structure with several roofs and lead-
paned windows.

"That's where you grew up?"

She couldn't stop herself from asking. Even at night
she could tell the home was a showplace.

"It looks bigger from the outside than it is."

Yeah, right.

Lights spilled out from a multitude of windows. The
house was at least three stories tall, and she would bet
there was a view of the ocean from the back side and
that it was spectacular, at least on a sunny day.

"Looks like she's up."

She swallowed back her surprise. Yes, she'd known

he came from money, but this was beyond anything she'd expected.

Why was he so broke?

"Hopefully, Dudley won't get anxious while I go in and talk to my mom."

"Do you want me to unload him? Put him in that big round pen over there?"

"No. That's okay."

"I can stay out here with him, then."

"No, no. Don't do that. Another few minutes in the trailer won't kill him. Come on inside and wait for your friend. My mom will have my hide if I leave you out here on your own, emergency or no. She's old-school. Raised me to be a gentleman, even during times of crisis."

As if illustrating his point, he slipped out of the truck and around the front to open her door. He even held out his hand to help her down, but for some reason she didn't want to slip her fingers into his own. She stared at them for the space of a half-dozen heartbeats, then took a deep breath before she gently clasped his hand. The last time they'd touched, when she hugged him outside of Dudley's stall, she'd felt so small next to him. She still felt that way. Her fingers were tiny compared to his.

The door to the home opened.

"Wes?"

Light fell to the ground, pooling at the woman's feet, but Jillian could see her clearly thanks to the glass sconces on either side of the double doors. Shoulder-length platinum-blond hair and a face unmarred by lines. Cowboy jumped out of the truck, back end swinging as he ran toward a woman he clearly adored, but she didn't reach out for him. She couldn't. She held something in her arms. A bundle of blankets or something.

"Mom," Wes said. "Are you okay? Are you sick?"

Wes's mother walked forward, and the bundle in her arms moved.

"I'm not sick, but you might feel queasy in a moment or two." She had eyes for only her son as she stopped in front of him. "Wes. Meet your daughter, Maggie."

HE WENT STRAIGHT to the liquor cabinet. His mom followed in his wake. Jillian… Well, he didn't know if Jillian had followed them into the house or not.

"Wesley Landon, don't you dare get drunk on me."

The liquor went down like a ton of sharp-edged lava rock. It knocked a little clarity into his frazzled mind. With a deep breath, he turned to face his mom.

"Okay, start from the beginning."

She held the sleeping baby out to him. He didn't want to take her. He felt as if he'd slipped into someone else's body. He could barely recall what his mother had told him. Something about Maxine arriving at the ranch, the baby in the backseat, and then leaving less than five minutes later.

"Take her," his mom ordered.

He held out his arms. She gently handed the child off to him. "Careful. Support her neck."

The exhaustion that had overwhelmed him during the long drive home had completely faded. He did as his mom instructed and placed a palm beneath the child's fragile head. "How old is she?"

"Shh," his mom soothed. "She's sleeping. And she's less than a month old. Probably about two weeks, if I don't miss my guess."

Two weeks? He did the math and his heart sank when he realized the tiny little face with the eyes closed in sleep above chubby cheeks might actually be his. The baby thrust her lips out as if somehow understanding his thoughts. Or maybe she'd had a bad dream. Did babies have dreams? He had no idea. Had no clue about anything baby related.

She'd been wrapped in a white blanket, so tight Wes couldn't imagine her being comfortable, but she slept like the dead even when he held her clumsily in his arms.

"Hi, Mrs. Landon. I'm Jillian Thacker."

Crap. He looked up in time to see Jillian walking forward with her hand out. He hadn't even introduced them.

"Mom," he said softly, "Jillian's a friend of Mariah's. Her friend's truck broke down in Red Bluff, so I offered to give her a ride home, only you had me so worried she insisted I come straight here."

"Jillian, hello," his mom said, smiling. "Nice to meet you."

They shook hands. Then Jillian glanced around. "I was wondering if I could use a phone. I don't have cell service and I'd like to tell my friend I'm here."

"Go ahead." His mom waved Jillian toward the back of the house. "It's in the kitchen. On the counter."

His gaze connected briefly with Jillian's, and he spotted the way her eyes caught on the bundle in his arms, but only for a brief moment because she looked away, quickly, as though uncomfortable with the sight of the child in his arms.

He didn't blame her. He held a baby. A *daughter.*

"How did this happen?" he heard himself ask.

"Well, I suspect approximately nine months ago you and that woman had sex."

"Mom." The baby stirred. His stomach lurched. What did one do when a baby grew restless? "I know how babies are made. How the hell did you end up with…?" He tried to remember the baby's name.

"Maggie," his mom finished for him.

Maggie. Her name was Maggie.

"Why did she leave her with you?"

"Sit down, Wes."

He realized that he'd started pacing when the poor baby's eyes opened. They were green. Startlingly, piercingly green.

"I don't understand." He met his mom's gaze. "Why didn't she tell me?"

"She said she tried to call."

"Yeah. Call. To tell me she needed to see me. But she'd been saying that since the day we broke up, and that was just about nine months ago, Mom, so she couldn't have been very pregnant." Well, she could have been, he supposed. "I mean, she couldn't have known so early. And when she did find out, why didn't she come to see me?"

"She said she wanted to wait until the baby was born. To be sure it was yours."

"Be sure it was… You mean she wasn't certain before?"

His mom appeared uncomfortable. "She said when she saw Maggie's eyes, she knew she was yours."

Wes closed his own eyes. She'd been cheating on him. He'd known that. It was why he'd broken up with her. Well, that and other things—like the fact that it'd turned out she was after his money. They'd met at a dinner for owners at the Turf Club—his mom had invited him. They'd dated for a couple of weeks, but once Maxine realized he was a lowly farm manager and that he didn't actually own Landon Farms, she'd gone a little crazy on him. He'd attributed it to her disappointment that he wasn't some kind of millionaire and had broken up with her over the whole thing. When she'd called him half a dozen times a day, he'd counted it a lucky escape.

"What am I going to do?"

His mom's face had softened. "If it's any consolation, I'm in just as much shock as you."

"Did she leave a number?"

His mom nodded. "She said to give her a call in the morning."

I'll bet, he thought.

"We should do a DNA test."

His mom nodded.

"But in the meantime…"

"What do we do with her?" his mom finished.

"I can help with that."

They both looked up to see Jillian standing there.

"I caught Mariah just as she was leaving. She's on her way over with some stuff. Crib. Changing table. Bathing tub. It was donated to CEASE for our annual rummage sale, but she's going to bring it here instead. What about diapers and formula?"

"The mom left us with a bag of supplies."

"Good. Wes, do you have a room you can use at your place?"

A baby. He had a baby. He just couldn't get used to the idea.

"He does," his mom answered for him.

"Let's go get it ready."

Chapter Nine

His mom was about to leave. Mariah and Jillian had already left, which meant soon he would be alone. A surge of panic made it nearly impossible to breathe. His hands shook as he gently set Maggie down in her crib.

"What if she wakes up?"

"She *will* wake up," his mom said. The light outside the room in the hallway allowed him to see the amusement in her eyes. "But I've made up some bottles of formula and left them in the fridge. Warm them up for thirty seconds at a time until they're lukewarm."

Warm them up? "What if I make it too hot?" he said, careful to keep his voice low. A glance into the crib revealed Maggie sleeping soundly, her face a pearlescent white in the muted half-light. "And what if she needs her diaper changed? What if she starts crying? How do I get her to stop?"

His mom was shaking her head. "With babies this age it's easy. They're either hungry, wet or wanting to be held. Try each thing until she stops."

She made it sound so simple. Wes had a feeling it was not, but he'd insisted on tackling this on his own. It wasn't his mom's fault he'd been a careless idiot nine months ago.

Stupid idiot, more like.

His mom stepped back from the crib, and he resisted the urge to beg her to stay, at least until he felt a little more comfortable.

Thousands of new parents deal with a new baby every day. You can, too.

Outside the baby's room, his mom gave him a kiss on the cheek. Jillian had promised to look in on him tomorrow. He'd heard her say something about working for a day care in a past life, although he hadn't been certain if she'd been serious about having a past life, or if it'd been a figure of speech. Once they'd dropped off the crib and other items, he'd waved goodbye.

"Call me if you need anything."

What he needed was a nanny. Or better yet, a different life.

You should have called Maxine back.

He should have done a lot of things. He should have not gotten involved with Maxine in the first place. Or maybe not gone to that party. Or used a damn condom. Damn it. What had he been thinking?

He heard the snick of the front door as his mom left. Should he go back in Maggie's room? Sleep next to her, maybe? Did parents do that? Maybe they should have put her in his bed. But what if he rolled over on her? Better for her to be in a crib, he thought, quietly slipping through the door even though he told himself to crawl into bed and try and get some sleep. Yeah, right. Like that would happen.

The little girl in the crib looked tiny against a maroon backdrop. They'd taken a queen-size sheet and wrapped it around the mattress a few times. His mom had brought him a matching fleece blanket, but Maggie lay on top, bundled inside her white blanket. Her little mouth opened and closed, as if she nursed on a bottle in her dreams. And it was funny because he'd done some pretty brave things in his life—cliff jumping in Mexico when he was younger. Paragliding on the same trip. Bungee jumping, too. But nothing filled him with as much fear as staring down at that little girl.

"I won't let you down."

But the truth was, he already had. He should have been with Maxine through the pregnancy. Should have taken her to her doctor's appointments. He should have held Maggie when she'd been born.

"I'll make it up to you," he whispered, wanting to touch her face, terrified to do so. "I promise."

Bright green eyes popped open. It felt like coming face-to-face with a tiger. She took one look at him and bawled…like a baby. Which she was. And he was absolutely panic stricken at the thought of picking her up. What if he dropped her? What if her head flopped back? What if the burrito blanket came undone? Would he be able to refasten it?

"Son of a—"

Ah-ah. No swearing.

He almost whipped out his cell phone to call his mom. She probably wasn't even back at the house yet. Besides, he had to take the plunge sooner or later. The little girl was his responsibility. Man, what a sobering thought.

His hands shook as he reached inside the crib. He managed to pick her up right, her little head supported in the palm of his hand, her tiny body as light as a feather.

"Shh," he soothed.

It was as if he played a part in a movie, but the reality really was as he'd seen on TV. The child fit in the crook of his arm. He peered down at her, smiled, gave in to the urge to touch her face.

"It's okay," he said. "I've got you."

The sobs faded. Eyes stopped squeezing out tears. The little wrinkled brow smoothed. Green eyes met his own, and he couldn't breathe for a moment.

He owned animals. Loved his dog. Took care of sick critters. But nothing, absolutely nothing, had ever prepared him for looking into the eyes of a tiny human being, one solely dependent upon him for food and love and support and, yes, a shoulder to cry on.

"You're going to be all right."

He had a lounge chair, one used to watch football and car racing on the odd occasion he found himself with some free time. He settled into it now, reclining it back with the flick of a lever. Should he lay her on his belly? Did she want to rest her head on his shoulder? Heart pounding, he gently moved her into position against his shoulder. No crying. If anything, it was as if her tiny little body went slack. He could feel it. Could hear her breathing slow. Felt her head get heavier. The smell of her, all baby cream and talc, made him close his eyes.

He could do this, he silently told himself, and it was one of the last thoughts he had before both of them— baby and father—drifted off to sleep together.

As a LIFE-ALTERING EXPERIENCE, it didn't get much bigger than a baby, Jillian thought on their way home.

"I can't believe the woman just dumped her kid on Wes's lap," Mariah said, swiping a lock of her crazy red hair—Disney hair, Jillian liked to call it—away from her face.

"Well, technically Wes's mother's lap," Jillian amended, stifling a yawn.

The highway was empty, and the hood of Mariah's white truck reflected the glow of sodium lights. She didn't know how Mariah could sound so chipper. Then again, as a veterinarian, she spent a lot of time helping ailing horses and their panicked owners. She was used to long nights.

"Thank goodness we had that crib," Mariah said. "Although I suppose the baby could have slept next to Wes for a night."

The poor man had seemed absolutely panicked at the thought of caring for a baby on his own. His mom had offered to watch the child at her place, but Wes had been insistent about caring for his own kid. She respected that. A lot of men would be only too happy to hand over their kids to Grandma…if the baby girl even was his kid. But whether he'd fathered the child or not, she couldn't believe someone would just drop the little girl off with near strangers.

"You sure you want to dive in and help him with that mess?" Mariah asked.

"I think he could use all the help he can get."

"And I thought *I* was a sucker for charity cases."

Her friend was. As the founder of CEASE— Concerned Equestrians Aiding in Saving Equines— Mariah had the biggest heart of anyone she knew. Ironic that she'd been trying to set her up with Wes for months.

"Poor Wes." She heard her say.

Jillian privately echoed the thought even as a part

of her wondered what he'd been thinking to have un-protected sex.

At least he was having sex.

She winced at the thought. She couldn't remember the last time. Actually, she could. She remembered it vividly. It'd been with Jason Brown...right before he'd announced he'd fallen in love with his leading lady, the one he'd ended up marrying a few months later. Proof positive that everyone made mistakes, including her. But this one would haunt Wes for the rest of his life.

She woke up the next morning wondering how he was doing. Probably still panicked, but it was hard to feel sorry for him as she pulled into Landon Farms. By the light of day the acreage reminded her of a bright green flag, one rolling in the wind. From the vantage point of the entrance it was easy to see how it angled down to the coastline. She couldn't see the house or the barn, but she could tell the place had to be worth a small fortune. The fencing alone must have cost a pretty penny. No wooden fence posts for Landon Farms. She'd been given the pass code last night. The iron gate made to look like crashing waves didn't make a sound as it swung back. Jillian's mouth dropped open in awe.

Granite stonework covered the front of the barn, and really, it wasn't just a barn but an elegant riding stable with an opening in the middle that she realized was an arena. Natalie would kill for a place like this, Jillian thought. What horse person in their right mind wouldn't want an equestrian facility like this?

Wes's home was tucked out back, around one of the small hills that cupped the valley. The single-story dwelling couldn't be seen from the barns, which meant it had its own scenic view of the mountains that stretched up from the coastline.

She heard the baby crying the moment she slipped out of her compact car. *Oh, dear.*

"Shh, shh, shh, shh." She heard him croon. "It's okay. I know you miss that miserable piece of you-know-what who claims to be your mommy, but I'm it for now, kiddo."

She didn't bother knocking. He wouldn't have heard over the baby's wails anyway. Cowboy was tucked near one of the bay windows at the back of the house, head between his paws, as if he were trying to cover his ears. The family room was right in front of the door, kitchen to her right, bedrooms beyond that. He appeared to be pacing between the kitchen and the family room, and he swung to face her when she entered.

"You look terrible," she said.

"I've been up all night. Well, not all night. I dozed off for a half hour or so, but then I woke up in a panic, terrified I'd dropped the baby. I kept doing that all night."

"I can tell." Because Wes Landon, the man who'd ridden a young gelding so confidently it'd been putty in his hands, appeared utterly and completely confounded by the young child in his arms. His eyes all but screamed the word *help.*

"Here," she said, holding out her hands. "I have some experience with this."

Her college job had been at a day care. She'd loved working with little kids nearly as much as she'd loved working with animals. "Come here, precious," she cooed.

He handed the baby to her as if it were a foreign object. "I got her to stop crying last night, but this morning? Nada. Zip. Zilch."

"I see you tried changing her." The poor thing's legs dangled down, the snaps that ran down the front of the onesie misaligned.

"I did change her, not that it helped."

"She's wet," she announced as she placed the child over her shoulder.

"How could she be? I just changed her a half hour ago."

His frustration was so evident she nearly laughed, even though the situation really wasn't funny. "They frequently pee after you change them."

"Says who?"

"The lady who owned the day care where I worked."

His expression suddenly resembled that of a man who stared at the holy grail.

"Thank God you know what to do." He turned to a pink bag sitting on the counter that ringed the kitchen area. "Do you have any idea how to roll them up in this?" He picked up the baby blanket. "Every time I do it, the darn thing comes undone."

She actually did laugh then. "I do. But let's change her first."

It amazed her how quickly it all came back as Jillian placed the baby on a blanket on the ground, the little girl's red face and watering eyes tugging at her heart. She'd always loved children, but she'd never have any. First there was the problem of needing a man, and these days, that was a long shot. Then there were the other little problems. Her vocation, which took her all over the place, sometimes for weeks at a time, not to mention her deep-rooted fear of loving something that much for the rest of her life. It would kill her if something happened.

"You're a pro," he said.

"Like riding a bike." When she finished, she motioned for the blanket. "Let's wrap her up and see if that helps. My boss used to swear that newborns needed the pressure of the blanket around them until they grew used to their arms and legs swinging free."

She glanced up in time to see him nod. In a matter of minutes she had little Maggie bundled up, and Wes warming a bottle. Five minutes after that, all was quiet.

"You're a godsend."

She looked up from feeding the little girl. "I'm just well trained. You'd be amazed how many diapers I've changed in my life."

She smiled. He did, too, and something in his eyes changed, a something that caused them to go soft and made her look away. What was with her?

"Have you heard from the mom?"

As a buzzkill, it worked like a charm. The green eyes so like Maggie's flashed. He shook his head. "I've tried calling, but I swear she dumped Maggie here on purpose, probably so she could go out and party somewhere."

"But you're pretty sure she's yours?"

His eyes had gone from soft to serious. "It's possible, Jillian. I'm not going to lie."

And it scared him. It would scare the crap out of her, too. She couldn't imagine suddenly discovering she was pregnant. Honestly, she'd have a nervous breakdown.

"You'll make a great father."

He wore a green shirt, one with dark blue stripes in a checkered pattern, the cotton fabric matching his eyes. His blond hair looked as if he'd brushed his hand through it a dozen times or more. He sat in a chair opposite her, but she noticed his jeans had spots on them, from the baby formula no doubt, and his eyes were red from lack of sleep. Still drop-dead gorgeous, but exhausted.

"Didn't you say you were going to ride Dudley today?"

It was his day off. She had a day off, too, since she'd originally been scheduled to be out of town until Saturday. It was why she'd offered to help. It was the least she could do after he'd been kind enough to drive her back to Via Del Caballo.

"I was going to, but now I don't know how I'm going to fit that in. Honestly, I don't know how I'm going to do much of anything anymore."

"You'll need to hire someone."

"I can't afford to pay someone to watch her full-time."

"Can't your mom?"

"I'm sure she could, but not all the time."

Cowboy came out of hiding, the dog shuffling forward and lifting his head.

It's a baby, she told the dog, flashing him an image of a puppy. The dog wagged his tail.

"He likes you."

She looked away, trying to hide her guilt. What would he say if she told him she talked to animals? He'd likely reach the end of his already frayed rope.

"He's probably curious about Maggie."

"I was worried he might get jealous."

"Nah. They understand that babies are human puppies."

"Are *what*?"

"Human puppies."

His mouth opened and closed a few times. "I don't know what's more strange, that you just called my baby—" She saw him mentally stumble over the word. "That you called Maggie a puppy, or that I bet you're right. I think they really do understand. Look at how he's wagging his tail."

Because she'd flashed Cowboy an image of a puppy and then another image of Maggie so the canine would understand...not that she could tell Wes that. Instead, she said, "When are you going to do a paternity test?"

"I don't know. That's something my mom is looking into. I think we need to find Maxine first."

"Maxine. That's the mom?"

He nodded. "I tried getting hold of her this morning, but she hasn't called me back."

She glanced down at the baby. She'd stopped suckling. "She's sleeping." She glanced up and smiled. "I think she liked listening to us talk."

"Or she needed a woman's touch."

"Maybe."

"Do you think she'd be okay in her crib for a nap?"

"I think you need to nap with her."

"No time. I told my mom I'd work today even though she insisted I take the day off as I'd originally scheduled. But I know how much she needs my help. The yearlings all need their supplements. I've got a horse being shipped out later today. Horses to turn out." He ran a hand through his hair. "It's a full-time job."

She'd been looking around his place as he talked, comparing it to the mansion on the hill. The two homes couldn't have been more different. His mom's house reminded her of a museum. Thick walnut furniture, gilded bric-a-brac, original artwork on the walls, all of it beneath vaulted ceilings framed with crown molding. This place was much more her speed. A few trophies on a mantel, the fireplace beneath ready for a match, based on the wood stacked on the grate. Photos next to the trophies. To her right a wrought-iron pot holder hung from the ceiling above the kitchen counter. Furniture worn but comfy.

"I don't understand why you have to work so hard." The question smacked of nosiness, but after seeing his mom's place, Jillian didn't get it. "Is your mom a miser or something?"

She'd pricked at an open wound, she could tell by his eyes. "It's not like that."

"Are you just really independent, then?" She was quick to add, "Don't get me wrong. I admire that, but there comes a point when everyone needs a helping hand."

He'd leaned forward, hands clasped, elbows resting on his lap. His green eyes narrowed. She had a feeling he mulled something over in his head, something important.

"She's not allowed to help me."

She couldn't hide her surprise. "Not *allowed*?"

Another long stare. "If I tell you something, you have to promise me you'll keep it to yourself."

She nodded. "Of course."

He took his time, framing his thoughts. "My family is wealthy. You know that."

"Really," she teased.

"Okay. I know." He smiled. "It's pretty obvious. But there's a reason why we're as rich as we are."

She had a feeling whatever he was about to say, it was a kicker. Something about the way he clasped his hands, his fingers twining together, his foot tapping the ground lightly.

"We…our family, I mean. My father and his father before him, they all had to make their own way in the world before they were allowed to inherit the Landon fortune. If I don't do the same thing, the whole thing, well, the majority of it, will be sold off and the proceeds donated to charity."

She felt her hair brush her cheek as her mouth fell open. "That's crazy."

"But effective. It's how we've held on to our wealth all these years.

She tipped her head sideways. "What do you mean by 'make their own way in the world'?"

"I mean earn a small fortune of their own."

"How much of a fortune?"

"A half a million dollars."

"Are you serious?"

"It's not as weird as it seems. It keeps the money out of the hands of family members who might squander it. My great-grandfather had an idea, you see. He thought that if his sons had to earn their own small fortune, they might be more appreciative of their inheritance. He'd watched a lot of great families go bankrupt thanks to one bad apple and he didn't want that to happen to his. So he came up with this, and it's worked so far. We've managed to increase our family fortune with each generation."

She tried to assimilate what he said. "So let me get this straight. Your family is rich, but you can't inherit any of that wealth until you make a small fortune of your own."

His eyes brightened when he said, "Yes. Exactly."

"Do you have to do it all in one shot? Is it something that accrues? What?"

"The money is held in trust. Every time I've won a purse on the cutting horse circuit, I've put some of it away. I was just about there when Bugsy bowed a tendon."

"Bugsy?"

"The best cutting horse I've ever owned. We were well on our way to earning that half million when he pulled up lame, so I guess you could say buying Dudley was a last-ditch effort to find a replacement."

"Good Lord."

"So you see now why I have so much riding on that horse you picked out for me."

"You're going to try and win the Million Dollar Cutting Horse Futurity, aren't you?"

He nodded his head. "On Dudley."

Chapter Ten

She stared at him as if he'd lost his mind. There were days when he wondered if he'd lost his mind, too.

"And if you don't win? What then?"

"I work for my mom for the rest of my life—not a bad proposition, really. She has some money of her own, and I'll inherit that, but this—" he motioned with his hands at the house and the ranch outside "—when my mom passes, it'll all be sold."

"That's barbaric."

"It's just the way it is. Everyone in the family grows up knowing about it. My dad has two brothers, but he was the only one of the three to earn his fortune. One of my uncles tried to challenge things when my grand-father died, but it couldn't be done. Turns out my great-grandfather paid a lot of money to some really great attorneys. I guess my grandfather did the same thing. My uncle James tried for years to get his hands on our family's wealth, but he couldn't. Kind of sad, really, because it caused a huge rift. I don't see my two uncles anymore. They refused to accept that they wouldn't be simply handed everything, but see, that's the beauty of it. My dad worked his ass off to make his fortune.

I've been working hard at it, too, and I'm close. One big purse is all it would take to tip me over the edge."

"But surely your mom could help."

"She could. She keeps telling me she'll sell me one of her top prospects cheap, but that would be cheating. If I'm going to do this, I'll do it without gaming the system…so to speak, even though my mother says it's no different from my grandfather Edward being sold a piece of land by my great-grandfather cheap and then reselling it later for a profit."

"She has a point."

"Maybe. But my grandfather still had to raise the money to buy that land. The fact that it turned out to be along the route of a future railroad was a stroke of luck, so I don't really look at it the same way."

She was shaking her head.

"What?"

"You're incredible." She bit her lip, clearly trying to work out what she wanted to say. And she looked so pretty standing there in an ivory-colored sweater with a scooped neckline, not at all like someone who trained horses. "I admire the fact that you refuse to take the easy way out." She glanced down at the baby in her arms. "Not with your daughter, and not with how you make your fortune." She met his gaze again. "It's rare to find a man with principles."

Their gazes held, and Wes thought yet again how remarkable her eyes were. It was just the two of them in the room, and baby Maggie, but it seemed as though they were the only people in the world, in the whole universe, maybe. She looked away as if knowing he studied her thoroughly and didn't want him to see too much.

"Yeah, I'm such a good guy I went and slept with a woman I barely knew."

She looked up again, but he noticed she didn't hold his gaze for long. "We all make mistakes."

"But this mistake might affect me for the rest of my life."

"And it might not."

It was true. They would do a paternity test to confirm he was little Maggie's father. Until then, who knew? Maxine was as flighty as a newborn deer. You never knew what she'd do. Witness how she'd dumped the baby in his lap—literally—something he would bet was a ploy. A way of getting his attention so she could get what she wanted out of him, which would be money, even though he'd explained to her over and over again that the money all belonged to his mom.

"The baby's asleep," she said softly. "I think we can put her down in her crib."

"To be honest, I've been half afraid to lay her down. I don't know anything about children. What if I do it wrong and something happens?"

Did he sound as panicked as he felt? Probably, because she shot him a reassuring smile. "Just don't lay her facedown. You'll see. Nothing will happen."

He followed her to his room, where they'd set up the crib the evening before. What he wanted to do was crawl into bed and take a nap, too, but he couldn't do that. Too much to do.

"There," she said quietly, laying the child down. When she straightened, their arms brushed, and Wes was about to apologize, but the expression in her eyes when she looked up at him made all the words in his head float away. There was a softness there, the same kind of softness as when she spoke about her love of animals, but gentler and somehow sweeter. The window at the rear of his bedroom had the curtains half-drawn, but her eyes were still the most remarkable color he'd ever seen, and from nowhere came the overwhelming urge to kiss her.

She felt it, too. He saw her eyes dip down, her gaze coming to rest on his lips. He lowered his head as a pristine stillness filled the room, but that stillness shattered into tiny little pieces when their lips connected.

She moaned. He lifted his hand to the side of her face and angled his head. He felt her straighten, thought she might draw away, but she didn't. She leaned into him instead, her mouth opening beneath his own. A million angels sang; a thousand church bells rang. That was what kissing her felt like. Never, not ever, had he experienced something so profound, so bizarre, so crazily, beautifully perfect as kissing Jillian Thacker.

"Knock, knock."

They jumped apart.

"Anyone home?"

His mom. Oh, jeez. He swiped a hand over his face and shook his head. He saw Jillian brush at her hair, smoothing the angular cut. Had he run his hands through it? He couldn't remember.

Quickly, he crossed to the door. "In here."

His mom had never been one for actually knocking, not even when he was a boy. She stood by the front door, a big bag, one the size of a Western saddle, in her hands.

"We just put the baby down for a nap."

He heard Jillian come up behind him. She must have gently closed the door, because he heard the snick of the latch. He saw his mom tilt a bit so she could see who stood behind him, but she was visibly disappointed to spot Jillian there.

"Have you heard from…her?"

No need to ask who "her" was. "No."

He noticed his hands shook, and not because of the mention of Maggie's mother. He wondered if Jillian had been similarly affected.

What the hell had just happened?

"I wondered whose car that was outside," his mom murmured, heading for the kitchen table.

"Hello, Mrs. Landon."

"Vivian," his mom said over her shoulder. "Please don't call me Mrs. Landon. It makes me feel so old."

Fortunately, his mom must have missed the signs that he'd just been kissing Jillian, because he didn't catch a "What have you been up to?" stare. Instead, she was busy unloading the contents of the bag onto the table.

"For goodness' sake, what'd you get?"

She glanced back at him wryly. "What *didn't* I get?" She held a package of pacifiers up. "Diapers, bottles, formula and out in the SUV, more stuff. Clothes and blankets and bath supplies. And a couple of bigger items. Playpen, stroller, high chair for later—"

"For later? Mom, we don't even know…"

He didn't finish the sentence. He didn't need to. They were all thinking the same thing, even Jillian, no doubt. The woman he'd just kissed probably called herself a fool for allowing a brand-new dad to kiss her. What a mess.

His mom must have read something of what he was thinking in his eyes. "I don't care whose baby it is, Wes. We need to take care of her." Her gaze moved to Jillian, but only for a second. "I assume you fed her before you put her down for a nap?"

"We did," Jillian answered for him. "I used to work for a day care."

His mom nodded in approval. "I worried I'd come back to find the poor little moppet starving, with a wet diaper and crying up a blue streak."

He resisted the urge to glance at Jillian, but he knew if he met her gaze, the memory of their kiss would come to the surface, a place where his mom might see it. He couldn't allow that to happen. Last night he'd insisted he and Jillian were friends. Last night he'd thought they were friends. And now that kiss. It'd thrown another stick in the fire of his life.

"Come on," his mom said. "You two help me unload the rest of the stuff while the baby sleeps."

"I THINK SHE bought the whole store." Jillian heard Wes mutter as he hefted another bag of...something out of the rear compartment.

"These look like groceries." She was trying to keep cool. Trying to act as if nothing had happened. Trying to appear as if she weren't inwardly screaming, *Ohmygosh-ohmygosh-ohmygosh.*

Wes shook his head wryly. "She does that from time to time. Buys me things so that I don't have to."

She'd kissed men before. Not a lot of them, but enough that she could compare her previous kisses with what it was like to kiss Wes. Not even Mr. Movie Star had caused the instant crescendo of want and need that Wes had aroused.

She looked up in time to catch Wes staring at her

strangely. She quickly tossed off, "Isn't that what moms are supposed to do?"

"I suppose so."

Okay. Focus. "You're lucky to have her."

He paused with his hands on another bag. "Do you have any family other than your aunt?"

"No." She sucked in a breath, trying to convey without words that she didn't feel sorry for herself. "And my aunt Linda died two years ago. Car wreck."

"I'm sorry."

"Don't be. I love what I do for a living and I have my little house and all the animals in the world. I'm very blessed."

Something had changed between them. No use denying it. He seemed to stare at her more deeply, more intensely, with more...understanding.

"You remind me of my mother." He picked up the bag, the plastic rustling. "She said pretty much the same thing after my dad died."

"Your mom is nice."

And every bit as beautiful as Wes was handsome. She had her son's blond hair, although hers had gone gray with age. She wondered if the resulting platinum color was due to good genes or a good hairdresser. Jillian couldn't tell. She had eyes the same color as her son's, too.

Eyes the same color as the baby.

That precious, adorable baby. The biggest reason of all she should not have, under any circumstances, kissed him back.

"She's the best mom in the world." He smiled as they headed for his front door. "She's also nosy, pushy and convinced I've lost my mind with this whole cutting horse thing."

He was trying to keep the conversation as normal as possible. She appreciated that. Jillian paused on the narrow porch that lined his home. Acres of green grass stretched up toward a highway hidden by rolling hills and dotted by cattle. In the distance the Santa Ynez Mountains sat brown and barren-looking compared to the coastal grasslands where they stood. She couldn't hear the ocean, but she could smell it, the salty tang of it causing her to wonder if they could ride to the beach. The proximity to the coastline made the land worth an absolute fortune, but she understood why Wes worked so hard to make his way in the world. Money was immaterial compared to the beauty of this place. She would have done anything to keep it, too, maybe even race a few horses. Well, okay, maybe not that. Like Wes, she had her standards. They had that in common, too—their love of horses, and that kiss...

"Speaking of cutting horses, I suppose I could put that stroller together and bring the baby with me while I ride."

"Don't be ridiculous."

They both looked up to find Wes's mother standing in the doorway, hands on her hips.

"The baby is still sleeping. You go do what you need to do today, Wes. I'll come get you if she wakes up."

Wes let the tall box that contained the stroller slide to his feet. "Mom. You don't have to watch her. She's my responsibility."

"And I'm your mother, and the child's grandmother." *Maybe.*

She didn't say the word out loud, but Jillian could read it in her eyes.

"Plus, you have a lot riding on that horse, Wesley. I'm anxious to see you get started. Go. Do what you need to do."

Jillian could see how torn he was by the way his lips pressed together and his fingers flexed as they held the white bag. His determination to be a responsible father warred with his desire to start training his new gelding and to carry out his duties as farm manager. Her estimation of him rose even more. When she'd first met him, she'd pegged him for a careless cowboy. Silver spoon in his mouth. Spoiled, probably. After watching how he reacted to his life being turned upside down and hearing what he hoped to accomplish, she realized nothing could be further from the truth.

"Can I watch you ride?"

What are you doing, Jillian? You already like him too much.

"Of course."

If you don't watch out, you'll end up liking him even more.

And that would never do.

Chapter Eleven

He'd wondered on the way home from the sale if he'd imagined Dudley's talent. It took ten minutes of working with the horse to realize that if anything, he'd underestimated the scope of his ability. After an hour of working cattle, he couldn't keep the grin off his face. Not just talented, the horse was gifted. He'd nearly come off a few times as Dudley ducked left and then right chasing a steer, legs close to the ground, the steer he held back from the herd crying out in distress.

"Easy, boy," he told the horse when he pulled him up. His black cowboy hat had become dislodged. He had to cram it back down on his head. "You're doing great."

The animal snorted and then shook his head as if saying, "Then let's keep going."

Dudley's copper coat had turned mocha-brown with sweat. He patted him again and said, "That's enough."

"He looks great."

It was his mom's voice. He hadn't even noticed her arrival, but there she stood, next to Jillian, outside of the massive circular pen his mom claimed she'd had built for her racehorses, but he knew better. Racehorses didn't need cattle chutes, but that, too, his mom had excused away. Made it easier to doctor the cattle they raised if they had a place to gather them. He hadn't been able to argue the point.

And then he spotted the stroller.

He'd been able to forget for a brief hour that he was a daddy. The anxiety returned to kick him in the gut. He'd tried half a dozen times to get hold of Maxine. She hadn't returned a single call. As he rode Dudley toward his mom, he wondered yet again if that wasn't part of her plan. Make him sweat. Keep him guessing what her next move might be. Manipulation. And it had worked.

"How is she?" he asked, trying to see over the rail of the arena to the tiny bundle inside.

"She woke up hungry, but we took care of her, didn't we, Cowboy?"

His dog glanced up at his mother, but only briefly. He kept his eyes on the stroller. Weird. He'd seen them before. Whenever there'd been children at a cutting event, he'd never given them a second look. But his dog seemed to know he had babysitting duty today.

"Did you need me to watch her for a bit?" Jillian offered.

Jillian. The whole time he'd saddled up Dudley, she'd asked if she could help him out, and when he'd declined, she'd taken it upon herself to pick up a rake and start mucking stalls. He'd told her no…and been firmly ignored.

"I can take her off your hands," Jillian added.

"No, no," his mom said. "She's fine right here." His mom reached through the rail, patting Dudley on the neck. "What's his name?"

"Dudley Dual Right," Jillian provided.

His mom laughed. He hadn't heard her laugh like that in a while. Things had been tough for her since his dad had died. Tough for him, too, but he always kept so busy. His mom tried to keep busy, too, but he could tell her heart wasn't in it. It didn't help that the clock continued to tick down toward his next birthday. He knew she worried about him, fretted over his future.

"How long have you been watching?"

"Ever since the arena came into view."

His house was tucked back, away from the massive stable where his mom bred and raised her racehorses. His home had originally been a caretaker's cottage, the stables built by a wealthy movie mogul in the 1930s and then refurbished by his dad when they'd bought the place. It was out of the way, around the base of a small hill, but he'd been so engrossed riding that he hadn't even noticed his mom strolling down the gravel drive.

"I think he might be as good as Bugsy." He stepped down. The dark brown chaps he wore had slipped down around the waist. He tugged them back up.

"Oh, Wes, really?"

Nobody could understand the importance of this little horse like his mom. His gaze fell on Jillian. Well, Jillian, too.

"How did you end up with him ahead of the sale?" His mom eyed the horse, her knowing gaze skating over the horse's narrow frame. They'd been so busy taking care of Maggie last night they hadn't even had time to talk.

"That's a funny story." He tugged the reins over Dudley's head. "Jillian told me to buy him."

"Really? Why?"

Jillian shrugged. "I just liked the looks of him."

"And then he bucked off his owner."

"He *what*?"

"The owner was an idiot," Jillian explained.

"But Jillian insisted I buy him."

"Are you a professional consultant or something?" his mom asked.

"Well, I'm a trainer first. I specialize in horses with difficult dispositions. I suspected Dudley's problems had more to do with who was riding him than being a bad horse."

"Like a horse whisperer or something." His mom seemed tickled by the concept.

"Something like that."

"Wow. We have a mare who has a horrible disposition. We're hoping to breed her, but I'm almost afraid for fear of what she might do to the foal. Maybe you could help us pinpoint what's going on."

Jillian eyes glowed. "I'd love to help out."

"In fact, I might have you look at all my racehorses." His mom turned to him. "I can't imagine it'd hurt, and it might actually help."

Just then the baby started fussing. He watched as both Jillian and his mom went to the side of the stroller, his mom cooing at the little girl. She might have aged in recent years, but she was still beautiful, especially when her whole face softened the way it did right then. Jillian had looked the same way earlier, but for some reason the two of them together, Jillian and his mom, shushing and kissing at the little girl, *his* little girl, it did something to him.

A cold nose brushed his hand. He glanced down and spotted Cowboy. The dog's tail wagged, as if he tried to tell him that he understood his master's fascination, that he felt the same way, too.

"Can I pick her up?" he heard Jillian ask.

"It's not up to me—it's up to Wes."

They turned to look at him, but was it up to him? Damn it. He wished Maxine would call him back. "Sure."

This was potentially the biggest year of his life, and Maxine's little stunt couldn't have come at a worse possible time. And yet the sight of Jillian lifting up Maggie, of the way she nestled the baby in the crook of her arm and then the way she cooed at the little girl some more, a smile on her face, it had him thinking for the first time that maybe this wouldn't be such a bad thing after all.

The thought stayed with him up until the moment Maxine called, and then just the tone of her voice told him nothing would ever be the same again.

"WHAT DID SHE SAY?"

It was a while before her son would answer. Vivian's appetite had completely faded the moment she'd heard Wes's cell phone ring and then spotted the tension that had spread across his face. He'd left the kitchen to take the call, but she didn't need to know what was said to know it wasn't good.

"She says the baby's mine and therefore my responsibility."

No demand for money? That surprised her. The moment the woman had arrived at her front gate, Vivian had known there was trouble. She'd met her at the racetrack on the night of the benefit, but Maxine had never been to the farm before. When she'd heard her name and recognized her on the security camera, she'd felt a kick to her gut. She would have never guessed what she had inside that vehicle, though.

"Well, if you're Maggie's father, she's right."

Wes took a seat at the table. In the distance the ocean sparkled like a million Christmas lights. They were eating early so they could put the baby down for the night at a reasonable hour. She glanced over at the bassinet she'd bought earlier, but not even the fact that the little girl was quiet seemed to calm her son's nerves. If she didn't miss her guess, not much would bring a smile to his face.

Poor boy. So much on his plate, and now this.

"She said if I don't take care of her, she'll put Maggie up for adoption."

Vivian wasn't much for swearing, but she felt like it right then. "Did you tell her you would never let that happen?"

"I told her. And she knew it before. It's why she dumped her here in the first place. I just wish she'd told me earlier what was going on."

Vivian wondered if this wasn't all part of some kind of plan. Get her son attached to Maggie and then threaten to take the child away unless Wes gave her money.

Her stomach churned just thinking about it. Their dinners lay in front of them, forgotten. Chinese stir-fry. From the smell of it, her cook had outdone herself.

"I suppose I'll have to call on Monday for a paternity test just to confirm it, even though I know she's mine."

"How do you even arrange for those?"

"I don't know. I suppose I'll have to call Dr. Starnes."

"In the meantime, I think it makes sense to have me look after her." She glanced at the bassinet. "She's less than two weeks old, Wes. She won't be much trouble."

"Mom, you're too old to be watching a baby."

"I am not too old."

"It's a lot of work."

"You don't think I know that?"

"It's my responsibility."

"Yes, but I'm here to help." She picked up her fork even though she wasn't the least bit hungry. In times like these it helped to go on as if nothing were out of the ordinary. When her husband had died, that was what she had done. One foot in front of the other. Breathe in. Breathe out. One day at a time. "Wes, you don't allow me to help enough as it is. Please. Just this once, accept my offer. You have no idea how much it's killed me to watch you slave away all these years."

Her one and only child peered up at her with sadness in his eyes. "It's for a good cause." He picked up his fork, too. She had to work to hide her relief. The boy needed to eat. "If I succeed, then all that Dad and Grandpa and Great-Grandpa worked for will continue on."

"It's a stupid policy." She shook her head again. "I told your father that when I first heard about it. It's stupid and outdated. These days there's any number of things you could do to keep the bulk of the Landon fortune intact."

"There is, but like Dad used to say, you can't argue with success. Dad didn't see any need to change it and if I succeed—"

"*When* you succeed."

He nodded once. "When I succeed, I'll do the same thing. And Maggie will have to prove herself one day, too."

"Both you and she will have the money I've saved up over the years. My own money isn't tied to your father and his fripperies."

"Fripperies?" He cocked a blond brow at her, and she thought that was better. He didn't seem as stressed. "Mom, you've been watching too much *Downton Abbey*."

"That's what this reminds me of. Something out of a British historical."

"Well, it is what it is."

That was what her husband used to say, too. She'd tried to get him to change his mind over the years, but he'd always insisted having to earn his keep had been the making of him. Hardworking. Outgoing. Not afraid to take risks—that had been her husband. One only had to look at Edward's brothers to see what happened when men rested on their laurels hoping for a handout. They had the same upbringing, but they'd turned out to be selfish, superficial wastrels, according to Edward. Her husband had been the most remarkable man she'd ever met. Just thinking about him made her heart grow heavy, but she reminded herself that she'd been left behind to help Wes.

"Well, I'm glad you had the sense to accept Jillian's help today."

"I don't think she would have let me say no, but she can't be here all the time."

"Wesley Landon, I am telling you right now that I am going to help you with the baby. And if I'm not around, I'm sure any one of the other ranch hands or their wives will help out. It takes a village to raise a child and you have one right here. No, no." She held up her hand. "I'm not taking no for an answer. If Maggie turns out to be yours, that means she's my grandchild. I'm only doing what any grandmother with a very large trust fund and too much time on her hands would offer to do. I don't want to hear another word about it."

He might pretend as though he didn't need her help, but she could see the relief in his eyes when he said, "All right. Fine."

"And I think you should let Jillian Thacker help out, too."

"Mom, I'm not going to hit her up for free day care."

"Not that way. I had to talk to Mariah about the CEASE fund-raiser we're holding here and she told me Jillian's been a big help with CEASE's rescue horses. From what I hear she's a huge asset when it comes to spotting potential problems."

"With any luck there won't be any problems."

He had a point. She almost—almost—told Wes about everything she'd heard, but her pragmatic son would have a tough time believing in animal communicators.

"Just the same, I'm going to invite her out to the farm tomorrow to look at Dolly, the mare I want to breed. I'll have her look in on you, too."

"Mom, you don't need to do that."

"I want to, Wes. I want to help you to succeed and if there's even a slim chance this woman can help, I'll take it. It's too important not to do everything we can to ensure your success."

"But—"

"Shush. I'll send her down in the morning."

She saw his lips twitch. "Why do I suddenly feel ten years old again?"

She got up from the table, scooping up her plate in the process. "Because you'll always be my baby." She glanced inside the bassinet and at the sleeping little angel inside of it. "Even when my baby has his own baby to care for."

Chapter Twelve

Even when my baby has his own baby to care for.

The words repeated inside Wes's head as he made arrangements for a paternity test. Maxine had sounded so certain that the child was his, and to be honest, he'd started to believe her. She'd even volunteered to take a test, too, something that would make the DNA typing easier.

Still, the day of the lab appointment, his hands shook as though he had low blood sugar. He'd never driven Maggie anywhere and, to be honest, the thought scared the bejeezus out of him.

"You ready, kiddo?" he asked the little girl. They were in his family room, Maggie on a blanket alongside the car seat. His mom had given him a quick lesson the night before. Actually, it'd been more like a journey of discovery for the both of them. "Hopefully, I'm doing this right."

Insert left leg through one hole. Right leg in the other. Snap the two plastic pieces together. There. Done.

He sat back and admired his work. Maggie looked more like a race car driver. She gurgled and cooed happily, as if she knew she was going for a ride. It made him smile. The plastic mobile his mom had bought to hang off the handle caught her attention. It put such a look of wonder on Maggie's face, Wes's grin grew. Her whole body quivered when one of the dangling bits moved, and Wes would swear her eyes smiled.

Next, the truck.

That, too, was accomplished with relative ease. The seat snapped into the base with a satisfying snick. He made sure the seat belt looked right. He had to take a deep breath before he climbed into the driver's seat. If he positioned his rearview mirror just right he could keep the car seat in his line of sight.

Keys. Ignition.

The truck's engine started instantly. He backed out of his driveway like a ninety-year-old man. His speed didn't improve much as he headed toward the lab his doctor's office had recommended. According to their family physician it would take less than forty-eight hours for results. The only delay might be mail. Apparently, they needed to send the samples back east for testing. It wouldn't be more than a week, two weeks max, before he'd know for certain if Maggie was his.

His heart began to beat faster the closer he got to the lab. When he pulled into a parking spot in front of the single-story building he had to take a moment to collect himself.

Why was he so scared?

He glanced at the car seat in the back. This was it. The moment of truth. There'd be no turning back once the test was in the mail.

The reception area was full of people. The lab was also a clinic to donate blood and so the people in the lobby were a blend of old and young, well dressed and poorly clothed, tense and relaxed. Fortunately, they took him right in. Wes clutched the car seat's handle, matching diaper bag bouncing against his back, as he was shown into a room with a curtained door.

"A nurse will be right with you."

He set Maggie down on a chair wedged into the corner of the room. Just a mouth swab, he reminded himself. That was all. Both he and the baby would need to have it done. Shouldn't take more than a minute or two.

"Okay, what have we here?" said a young female nurse wearing a smock with Looney Tunes characters all over it.

"DNA test," Wes said, even though the woman had a piece of paper in her hand that no doubt told her what he needed done.

"Okay," she said with a professional smile that didn't reach the brown eyes that matched her hair. "Let me get set up."

He didn't know why his mouth suddenly went dry. Maybe it had something to do with the cotton swab about to be inserted between his lips. A big cotton swab. It was currently ensconced in a plastic tube with a label on the side. They would put *that* in little Maggie's mouth, too?

"Okay," said the woman after she snapped on gloves. "Here we go." She had short-cropped hair and a mole on her cheek that Wes found himself focusing on when she said, "Open wide. I'm going to swab the inside of your cheek. Just relax."

Easy for her to say. She wasn't the one about to be jabbed with a big-ass Q-tip. He glanced at Maggie sitting in her portable car seat so peacefully.

Sorry, kiddo. Your turn next.

It wasn't painful, just uncomfortable. "Okay. Done." Yet another fake smile. "Baby next."

His stomach dropped. He might not know a whole bunch about babies, but he doubted Maggie would like the stick any more than he did.

"Do you need me to take her out of her seat?"

"Nope. She's fine." The nurse slipped his sample in the plastic tube, snapped a lid on it, and then wrote something on the side. She turned toward Maggie when she was done. "Open wide," she told the baby.

"I really don't mind holding her."

"Nope." She didn't even glance up at him as she squatted down. "This is fine."

She had the tone of "just leave me alone and let me do my job," and Wes's hackles rose. This was his daughter…maybe, he had a right to be concerned.

"She might feel better—"

The nurse stuck her finger in Maggie's mouth, and if he hadn't been so concerned, he would have laughed at the way the baby's eyes bulged just before her face scrunched up in a way that clearly conveyed her distaste for having a rubber-tasting finger stuffed inside. Two seconds later she let out a huge cry. The baby tried to move her head, but the nurse deftly followed. The cry turned into a wail and the wail into the most heart-wrenching sound of distress Wes had ever heard. He lunged for her at the same time the nurse removed the swab.

"Hey, hey, hey," he said, brushing past the woman quickly. "It's okay. I've got you."

He didn't know how he unclicked the harness so fast, but he did, pulling Maggie up next to him before he could think twice. "Easy now. I've got you."

Maggie was furious. And outraged. And clearly felt betrayed. He could see all those emotions and more as he pulled her into the crook of his arm. "Shh, shh, shh."

"You should have results no later than next week." The nurse barely smiled as she placed their tubes in a plastic bag. "Call if you have any questions."

That was that. Over. Done. Not for Maggie, though. He ended up putting her over his shoulder, bouncing her and patting her, just as he'd watched his mother do.

He wanted to kill the nurse.

The emotion took him by surprise. He didn't even know if Maggie was his, but it didn't matter, he realized. She was his responsibility, and the nurse's callous disregard infuriated him beyond disbelief.

She's just doing her job.

He knew that, too, but it didn't make him feel any better. From the moment Maggie had entered his life he'd promised to keep her safe. And now he'd let some stranger jab at her mouth.

"It's okay. She's gone." Maggie's cries started to wane. "I promise. All done."

When he shifted the little girl back to the crook of his arm, his heart did something weird. The sight of her red-rimmed eyes, of the tears on her cheeks, of her flushed cheeks…it aroused something within him, something primal and powerful.

"You okay?" he murmured, stroking her cheek.

She blinked up at him, all soft eyes and sweet cheeks, and he knew that even if she turned out to be somebody else's, he would still want to keep tabs on her. The little girl had quickly stolen his heart. "We've got it all worked out, don't we?" he cooed to the little girl, deciding to change her diaper. With one hand, he moved the car seat off the chair, grabbed the paisley-printed blanket he'd tucked against her and set it on the chair then he gently laid her down. "You're not so scary."

He fished in his bag for a diaper before removing the old one. The strip of tape went right above Elmo's head on the diaper, the other one above Ernie. It'd taken him three days to figure that out. Three days of destroying one diaper after another because he'd taped it too loose or too tight or crooked.

"And there we go." He tickled her belly, smiling and bending his head down as if he might give her a raspberry.

She smiled back. He froze. The smile faded.

He had to be imagining things.

He tickled her belly again, this time actually blowing a raspberry, and when he straightened, there it was again. Unmistakable.

His heart melted.

How could she do it? How could Maxine leave her behind?

Out partying it up, no doubt.

Whatever.

He couldn't leave the lab quickly enough. Maggie settled into his truck quietly. He had a feeling her crying jag had tired her out because by the time he pulled into his mother's driveway, he was pretty sure Maggie was out. That worked out perfectly because he had chores to do.

"How was it?" his mom asked when he walked into her house with Maggie in tow.

"Horrible. But it's done."

His mom smiled at him in sympathy. "Just keep her in her seat. She'll be fine like that."

"Thanks, Mom."

"Jillian will be down later. She knows which horses I want looked at."

Jillian.

True to her word, his mother had hired her as a consultant. She'd been invaluable, too. He'd forgotten what it was like to have someone on the ground, helping him, giving him suggestions. She was a hell of a horse trainer with a genuine gift for spotting problems, he thought as he walked down to the stables. When he'd had trouble with Dudley's left lead, she'd told him it was because he was sore in the back. She'd recommended some ice and magnetic therapy, and presto, Dudley had gotten better. He'd been so grateful, had enjoyed her company so much, he'd had to fight the urge to kiss her again at least a half a dozen times. One thing stopped him. He was in no position to embark upon a romantic entanglement. Single dad. New baby. No future. Well, that wasn't true. As his mom had said, he'd always have a job. It just wouldn't be the future he wanted.

"You look deep in thought."

He glanced over at Jillian, brush in hand. He'd just finished riding and was giving Dudley a good grooming. Cowboy, who sat in the barn aisle, had apparently heard her approach. He took off with his back end wagging, his canine grin hard to miss.

"I was just thinking about my mom and what a big help she's been."

She had come in from the side of the barn opposite the sun. Light bathed her body, the golden glow catching her eyes and turning them the color of rain forest moss. She wore an emerald-green shirt that hung past her hips, one with a scooped neckline and long sleeves.

With no bling or designs on the front the top wasn't fancy, but on her nothing would ever be plain. With her high cheekbones set to advantage by her sharp black haircut, and her small chin, she couldn't have looked more gorgeous.

"Your mom is great," she said, reaching down for Cowboy and giving the dog a scratch. "She made Mariah's day when she agreed to help with our CEASE fund-raiser. It's been a goal of Mariah's for years to do something like this, and now here we are, but if you'd told me a year ago we'd gain the cooperation of an evil racehorse owner, I'd have never believed it."

"We're not all bad."

Her eyes swept over his face. "No, you're not."

Why did it feel as if she'd meant him? He turned back to his horse. He'd just finished his ride, and Dudley was tied in the middle of the barn aisle. He hadn't even heard her drive up. Not surprising given the size of the stable where he worked. He'd seen plenty of racing stables in his lifetime, and Landon Farms was pretty spectacular. The left side held a double row of twelve stalls, each made of dark oak, and each with black vertical bars across the top. The other two-thirds of the stable held an arena. His dad had renovated the place years ago and so everything was state-of-the-art, right down to the rubberized footing in the arena and the sliding stall doors where they housed their younger stock and mares due to foal.

He tipped his cowboy hat back so he could see her better. "How does he look?"

"Good." She smiled. "I'm sorry I missed your ride."

"No worries. It was just a bunch of the same stuff."

Funny how they'd never met until the gelding sale

and yet they traveled the same circles. He was glad his mom had volunteered to help. She had a soft spot for horses and the money to help them.

"At least I got to cuddle your adorable Maggie." Her smile slipped a little. "Your mom said the DNA test was horrible for her."

His. Yes, it had started to feel that way. Despite his absolute terror in the beginning, his tiny little girl had wedged herself under his skin. Maybe that was Maxine's plan.

"It was, but she got over it quickly."

As if reading his mind, she asked, "Any word from Mad Max?"

He nodded. "We're supposed to meet next Wednesday because she misses her baby girl. Forgive me for being skeptical, but I suspect she's suddenly claiming to miss Maggie because I haven't called begging her to help me take care of her."

Jillian nodded. "She wanted to put you over a barrel."

"Think so. I also think she thought my mom was a socialite or something—someone who wouldn't help me with Maggie's care, which just goes to show you how little she knows about me."

"Yeah. Your mom was great with her today. Maggie is lucky to have you both."

And there it was. The same look he'd seen on her face the day they'd kissed. The glimmer of admiration mixed with approval. She needed to stop staring up at him like that. It made him want to kiss her all over again.

"Anyway," he said, beginning to brush his horse once more, "I guess when we meet, I'll know more."

She came up and placed a hand on Dudley's neck, ran it beneath his mane and down toward his shoulder.

She pressed as she went along, looking for sore spots, her hands gliding up, along the ridge of his shoulder and down his back.

"He feels great." She smiled. "And he looks great, if you don't mind my saying. I know you've only had him for a short while, but I swear he's already picked up weight and filled out a little."

Funny how her nod of approval could make his spirits lift. "I thought so, too, but I told myself I imagined things."

"No. I think you're right."

They both stood back and admired the gelding secured in place by two red leads, one attached to the left side of the barn aisle and the other attached to the right. Dudley pricked his ears forward as if knowing they studied him and wanting to look his best. Silly horse.

"When's your first competition?"

His stomach lurched in excitement. "At the end of this month."

It was February, the cutting horse competitions a bit sparse this time of year. Heck, compared to recent years, there weren't nearly as many competitions. Nor was there the money. Big purses were hard to come by, so he'd picked something small. Not a lot of big-name trainers. Just something to get his feet wet.

"Can I come watch?"

He couldn't keep the smile from his face. "Of course."

He turned back to the groom box hanging from the wall. Their colors were yellow and black, something his dad had come up with: sting like a bee. The color scheme dominated their blankets, halters and saddle pads. The mailboxlike storage container he reached into was no different. The initials L.F. were painted on the front in black. He reached for a currycomb, then went to work on Dudley's coat. Quiet settled around them. It was like that with her. No need to fill the silence with chatter. He'd never felt more comfortable with someone in his life.

"Are you nervous?" she asked.

"A little."

"Honestly, Wes, you're going to do great. He's a winner."

"I think he might be, too." He patted Dudley's neck. "I traced his pedigree last night while I was waiting for Maggie to go to sleep. Everyone knows his sire's bloodlines, but his dam's pretty remarkable, too. Here, I'll show you." He unclipped Dudley and put him back in his stall. "It's up at the house. I went back ten generations. He's got a lot of foundation blood mixed in with Dual Rey."

She followed him from the barn. His mom's house was on the right, wooden corrals directly across the road from them. In the middle of the turnaround driveway a patch of grass sprouted, spring bulbs already making an appearance.

"It's so beautiful here."

"I know." He glanced down at his dog, who paced alongside of them. "Come on, Cowboy, let's give the lady a ride."

He drove a golf cart to and from his house. Made things easier. Jillian climbed in next to him. His ranch house was less than a half mile from the barn. His mom had planted bulbs along the road, too. In the springtime there would be orange poppies and daffodils dotting the roadside.

"I can see why you'd do anything to keep it."

He could tell she genuinely understood his love for

the land. The smile she gave him was once again soft and full of approval. He didn't know why, but he very much appreciated her approval.

Careful.

There he went wading into the deep end again. Didn't matter how many times he told himself he couldn't think of her that way—every time Jillian stood near he wondered what it'd be like to get to know her better, *intimately* better. Not even her weird psychic stuff bothered him anymore. Not much, anyway.

There were bulbs sprouting by the house, too, along the front of the narrow porch that ran the length of his house. Well, not his house, not really, but he didn't want to think about that right now. Instead, he called to Cowboy as they left the golf cart and then climbed the three steps to his porch.

He headed to the kitchen and the piece of paper that he'd left on the counter.

"Check it out." He slid the paper down the counter to her. "I knew Colonels Smoking Gun went back to Leo and Three Bars. But look at his dam. Joe Reed. Top Deck and, of course, Dual Rey. He's foundation bred through and through."

"That's so exciting."

The face she turned up to him should have lit the room, it glowed with so much excitement. It pleased her to know he was satisfied, and not for her own personal gain. He would bet his custom-made spurs that she would never advertise her part in his selection of Dudley. All she wanted was for him to succeed.

It humbled him, that support. Humbled and filled him with gratitude and made him want to do something he knew he shouldn't.

"Thank you," he said quietly.

He saw her still. "For what?"

"For being you."

He didn't want to do it. If he guessed correctly, she didn't really want him to kiss her, either, and not because she wasn't attracted to him. Their physical awareness of each other electrified the air. No. Her reluctance stemmed from the same internal misgivings that he echoed. Yet neither of them moved.

"What is it with you?" he asked. "I keep telling myself to stay away, but I can't seem to get you off my mind."

He saw her swallow. "Me, too."

His fingers had found her jawline, and he marveled at how soft she was.

"Do you have magic powers, Jillian? Because I feel as if I'm under a spell."

He could feel her breath on his hand. It fell with greater and greater frequency as he stroked the side of her neck. Vanilla and berries. The smell of her sweetness made him lean toward her.

"If I did have powers, I'd cast a spell to ward you off."

"And I'd break that spell." He couldn't take it anymore. "With a kiss."

Her eyes sprang open. His lips captured hers. It was like the last kiss but different. No more tentative exploration, just pressure and heat and then the soft glide of her tongue passing between his lips and then...heaven.

If she was a witch, surely she had him charmed.

Her mouth opened. The tips of their tongues brushed, once, twice, and then he angled his head and stormed the soft defenses of her mouth. A thrust and a parry and then a returning prod of her own tongue, and meanwhile they drew closer and closer until they were chest to chest and hip to hip and thigh to thigh and Wes knew she fought a losing battle.

She pulled her head away.

"We can't."

"I know."

"It'd be stupid."

"I don't care."

Her gaze flicked upward. The heat in his eyes was her undoing. "I don't, either."

Chapter Thirteen

He took her hand and led her out of the family room and toward his bedroom. Already a tightening had begun in his groin, one that spurred him on and made his steps quicken as he headed down the hall. She didn't resist, not even when he paused for a moment before the bedroom door, or when he opened that door and revealed a room decorated in browns and beige with the bed to the right. When he turned to face her near the edge of his bed, he was struck by her beauty. Her eyes. They were the color of moss after a new rain, a bright green that fascinated him with its intensity. But it wasn't just the color of those eyes; it was what was in them, too.

"You're so beautiful." He touched her cheek again. "On the inside." He marveled for a moment. "Your goodness glows from your eyes."

She covered his fingers with her own. "That's the sweetest thing any man has ever said to me." She leaned her head into his hand. Like a kitten, kissing his fingers, the touch of her lips sending tingles up his arm and through his body. He leaned down, pulled her up against him with his other hand and kissed her again. That same hand dropped, finding and then tugging up her shirt. When his palm made contact with bare skin,

he knew there'd be no turning back. Touching her skin
made all his nerve endings fire. Made him kiss her
more deeply. Made him lift the shirt up higher until
he reached the edge of her bra, his fingers slipping beneath the lacy fabric.

She gasped.

He'd found the swell of her breast but it really wasn't
what he wanted to do—touch her there—and so he
leaned back and lifted her green shirt. It came off with
an ease that made him sigh half in relief and half in admiration because she had one of those athletic bodies,
the kind with a flat belly and a narrow waist.

"Gorgeous," he murmured just before his lips lowered to the curve of her breast. His cowboy hat brushed
her collarbone. He tossed it aside and lowered his head
once again, fingers tugging at the fabric of her bra.
When his mouth found her dusky center, she sighed,
too, but for a different reason. Hers was a sigh of satis-
faction and of surprise and of need.

"Wes." He heard her say as she arched into him.

She tasted sweet and warm and like the berries he
always smelled whenever around her. Her hands found
his hair, the soft touch of her fingers prompting him to
be more bold, to lightly nip her. Her hands moved, too.
He understood why a moment later. His denim shirt
began to slide upward. He angled his shoulders to help
her ease it off. They moved as one toward the edge of
the bed and it took everything Wes had not to pick her
up and place her on the mattress. She grasped the top of
his jeans. He paused for a moment, giving her the op-
portunity to stop, not wanting to pressure her. Instead,
she released the pressure inside his pants by unsnap-
ping his jeans. Her knuckles brushed the ridge of flesh

covered by his boxers. He hissed, and when her mouth found his own nipple, he sucked in a breath. She was shorter than him by a lot, and so she didn't have to move much to do things to him, amazing things...

She unbuttoned her pants. He felt more than saw her do it and by the time he opened his eyes, she'd let them drop and they were standing there almost naked and he went back to kissing her again, only this time there was a sense of urgency to it. He lost strength in his knees. She did, too, both of them falling onto the bed. She landed on top of him, and he liked that she took the initiative. He would have kept on kissing her, except he sensed something. A canine something. He turned his head.

Cowboy stared at them.

He froze. Jillian must have sensed it. She turned, too.

"He thinks we're playing."

"Oh, we're playing, all right."

She laughed. He snapped his fingers. Cowboy glanced back and forth between them and Wes could tell he really did think they were playing. He had a silly canine grin on his face.

"Go lie down," he told the dog. The silly canine grin dimmed. "Go on."

She collapsed against him, but for a different reason this time. She was laughing.

"What's so funny?"

"Nothing."

Something had tickled her funny bone, but he didn't care what, because he was entranced with what amusement did to her face. He placed a palm against her face, the two of them eye to eye. She still wore her bra and her underwear and he couldn't help but think she looked like a sexy lingerie model with her chic hairstyle and unusual eyes.

"I'm surprised men don't beat a path to your door." His fingers skated along her cheek. "You're so beautiful."

The amusement faded away. She blinked a few times. He didn't know what emotion he saw in her eyes, but he didn't like it. He leaned up on an elbow before bending and kissing her. She didn't move at first, and for a moment Wes worried that something had changed, that whatever it was he'd seen in her eyes had scared her. But then she kissed him back. Hard. Her hands shifted to the back of his neck, holding him there, her body arching into him. It was all the answer he needed. He hooked a finger into his waistband, slid his boxers down. She somehow managed to keep kissing him while shrugging out of her bra and underwear.

Still, he had to ask, "Are you sure?" as he opened his nightstand drawer.

"I'm sure."

Her eyes never looked away from his own, not when he opened the foil packet, not when he slipped protection on, her gaze unwavering as he slid between her thighs.

He thought they'd lose themselves in a kiss again, but when his lips touched hers, it was only momentarily. He shifted a bit, kissed her once more, briefly, just a light touch. With each kiss her eyes grew softer, and with each nudge of his hips, those remarkable eyes of hers changed. He was mesmerized.

Her hand found his. Their fingers twined. When at last their bodies joined, she released a sigh. He did, too, but he couldn't look away from her, didn't kiss her again, just marveled at what it felt like to be inside her while their gazes held.

She tipped her chin and, when he thrust, kissed him, hard, mouth open, tongue searching. He moved again and she withdrew. Another thrust and she went back for another kiss. He groaned. She did it again, pulled her lips away when he pulled away. He thrust deeper. She kissed him deeper. The erotic tease drove him nuts, and yet he'd begun to climb and so had she. He could see it in her eyes. He thrust again and she kissed him again, and then he closed his eyes because he knew he wasn't going to last if he kept staring at her.

It didn't help.

They'd connected, not just physically but emotionally, too. He didn't need to see her to feel her, to anticipate her moves, to find her mouth. He didn't need to look in her eyes to know they were full of want. His climax hovered. So did hers, but he held them there, wouldn't let them crest the rise, slowed things down for as long as he could, only he couldn't seem to stop it from happening. A light flashed. The world moved. He cried out. She did, too.

"Wes."

Jillian, he answered back silently. *What have you done to me, Jillian?*

His hands squeezed hers, Wes surprised to realize their fingers were still twined. His forehead rested against her shoulder as they ever so slowly returned to earth.

She'd bewitched him, that was what she'd done, and God help him, Wes wasn't certain he could ever break her spell.

Chapter Fourteen

She wanted to stay in his arms all day. Wanted to go on pretending his house was a perfect oasis, a place where they could keep reality at bay. A place where there were no crazy ex-girlfriends, where she didn't have to be afraid Wes would break her heart, where she was like any other normal person, one who didn't fear falling in love.

Could she love Wes?

She turned her head. His green eyes were full of softness and delight, her own lids suddenly heating up as if she might cry.

Yes, she probably could.

"I better go."

His brows lifted. "What?"

She slid sideways off the bed, calling over her shoulder, "Your mom's going to wonder why I'm not working with her horses."

The bed shifted. She knew he'd sat up, too, a hand landing on her shoulder before his lips lightly grazed the back of her neck. "She probably thinks we're still down at the barn talking about Dudley."

She might. Then again, she might not. What if the woman had gone down to the barn to check in on her?

Vivian was no fool. She'd know with a glance what had just happened.

Damn it. Where was her bra?

She found it at the foot of the bed. Her shirt, too. She quickly pulled them on.

"You sure you don't want to stick around?" He reached out and picked up his shirt, but he didn't slip it on. "I have to feed the horses and check water. I thought you might want to tag along."

A part of her longed to say yes. Another part of her, the sane and logical part, told her to get away fast.

"I'd like to, Wes, I really would, but I want to see how that broodmare is doing. Plus, Natalie's away at a show this weekend, and I promised I'd pop in and check on her horses tonight which means I don't have a lot of time to spare." Which wasn't precisely true. She'd told Natalie she'd drop by at some point this weekend, but it didn't have to be today.

"Too bad."

Yes, she thought, putting on her pants. Too bad. It was all too bad.

"Will I see you this week?"

"I don't know. Depends."

Vivian had asked her to look in on her horses at Golden Downs racetrack. Plus she had a few new clients and then her regulars. "Busy week."

He'd gotten dressed as quickly as she had, moving around the foot of the bed and stopping in front of her. "I feel like you're running out of here."

She hoped he didn't see the way his words made her want to look anywhere but at him. She *was* running. Her heart even raced as if she'd just run a marathon. "I'm just in a hurry to get back to the barn."

"Are you worried my mom might be down there looking for us or something?"

"Actually, yes."

He smiled then shook his head. "She's not, and even if she was, she wouldn't care what we've been up to."

She wasn't so sure. "I just worry she might not approve. You know, especially with all that's going on in your life."

It was the right thing to say. He nodded, and she noticed that his hair had a crease in it where his cowboy hat had been. For some reason she found that adorable.

Get out now.

"We'll talk later." She had to just about jump up to kiss his cheek. He reached for her, but she ducked away before he could catch her. The pulse at the base of her neck felt like a woodpecker.

"You want to try for dinner tomorrow, then?"

She kept walking. "Can't. I'm supposed to go over to Mariah's house tomorrow and work some more on the benefit."

When she glanced back, she could see the disappointment in his eyes. Better this way, she told herself. Keep it casual. He was a man. They were used to that type of thing. He had a baby because of that type of thing.

She paused by the front door, then looked back again. Wes stood in the hallway, shirt off, Cowboy at his feet. The sight of the two of them standing there, both of them staring at her so intently, it made her wonder what would happen if she threw caution to the wind and let her heart fall.

"I'll call you." It sounded so trite and so cliché, so… dismissive.

He reached down and patted the top of his dog's head. "Drive carefully."

Coward.

No. She wasn't a coward. She was pragmatic. It was easier this way. They barely knew each other. Their being together was just…chemistry. Nothing more.

But with every step she took, regret built. It filled her to the point that she almost felt ill as she went first to the barn to check on Vivian's broodmare and a few other horses then later walked back to his mother's home.

"There you are."

Vivian. She was out front, kneeling in a flower bed, a baby monitor a splotch of white in the grass.

Damn. She'd been hoping to slip out unnoticed. "Sorry." She smiled. "I got hung up talking to Wes."

Vivian seemed to swallow the explanation. She got up and tugged off her garden gloves, the flash of her ring catching the quickly waning light. "I was hoping to catch you before you left. I had an idea while you were visiting with my son."

Visiting. That was one way to put it.

"I thought, why don't we hold that benefit we talked about here at the house?"

She was so busy wondering if Wes's mother suspected what had really gone on that she didn't catch her meaning at first.

"What?"

"The CEASE benefit." A smile sprouted on her face, one as large and as cheerful as a sunflower. "I was thinking about it after you left and I thought, wouldn't it be something if we held the benefit here at the farm? I mean, wouldn't that knock a few people for a loop. A benefit at a race farm for the organization that's made such a fuss at the racetrack?"

She referred, of course, to her friend Mariah's efforts to stop horse racing at Golden Downs, and she was right: it would be something. Definitely media worthy.

"Are you sure you want to do that?" No doubt she'd ruffle a few feathers. "I'm sure we can find somewhere else."

"You could, but why?" Vivian's smile was warm and full of self-satisfaction. "Ever since Edward died, I've been rattling around this place all by myself. It's too big for one person, but it's perfect for entertaining."

It was more than perfect. "I know, but—"

"Stop. I know what you're going to say. It's too much work, and with the baby." She glanced at the monitor on the ground. "But I'm good at entertaining. It's what I do best. Let me help you guys."

And what could she say to that? "Thank you, Vivian. Your generosity is incredible."

"Nonsense." She glanced up at the sky, her eyes going from deep green to light emerald. "We're losing daylight. I should probably call it quits for the day. Come back to the house later this week, maybe Wednesday. We'll start planning."

"I'll check with Mariah and see if she's available."

"If she's not, you and I can get started," Vivian said, her expression brightening in such a way that Jillian knew she liked her friend. "This will be a hoot."

A hoot. Being forced to see Wes? She'd decided on her walk that it'd be best to keep her distance from him. Now this.

"We don't have to meet. We could always use email."

Vivian's blond brows rose. "Don't be silly. Come by the house on Wednesday."

She couldn't say no, and so she didn't, but as Jillian drove home that night, she wondered how the heck she would avoid Wes. And why it seemed so important to do exactly that.

SHE WAS AVOIDING HIM.

It was easy to do. She'd handed out cards at the bull-and-gelding sale and between her existing clients and new ones, including Wes's mother, she'd been run ragged. She also maintained a blog, worked on a book she was trying to write and basically kept herself busy, but by Wednesday night she'd edged closer to the lip of the cliff. All day long she'd wanted to call Wes to see how his meeting with Maggie's mother had gone, but she'd stopped herself at least a half-dozen times.

Wednesday dawned after a fitful night spent dreaming of Wes. He'd been kissing her again. Doing that thing they'd done when they'd made love. She'd woken up sweating, anxious and out of sorts. She didn't know how she'd hide her anxiety from Mariah. When they'd met with Vivian a few days ago, they'd taken separate cars. Today they were riding together.

"You look great!" her friend said after rolling down the window to her state-of-the-art veterinary truck. A recent purchase that was all her own, instead of the one she'd been driving, which had been owned by the new clinic where she worked. Her own wheels, she'd told Jillian the day she'd bought it. "I love that outfit."

Had she overdone it? She wore a long-sleeved shirt with a studded cross on the front. A little more bling than usual, but the jeans were of the plain-Jane variety.

"Thanks. You look like you just got off from work."

"I did."

"But your hair looks different. Did you get it cut?"

She'd never seen her friend so happy. Her eyes glowed like a new piece of jewelry. The red hair, always wild and unkempt, had been tamed today. Instead of ringlets there were big curls.

"Oh? Do you like it? Zach and I are going out to dinner after our meeting with Vivian. You should see the dress I have stashed in the back. Very hubba hubba. Can't wait for Zach to peel it off me."

"Eww. I didn't need to hear that." But her friend's comment brought back memories of Wes's hand slipping beneath her bra—

Don't.

She didn't want to go there. So far she felt as if she'd gotten off lightly. Wes had tried calling her a few times, but she'd managed to duck every one of his calls, returning them when she knew he'd be busy feeding the horses or riding or taking care of something. She'd been lucky. She probably wouldn't be lucky tonight. But what did she say to him? "Sorry, Wes, but I think seeing you again is a bad idea"?

That's exactly what you should do.

She knew that, but it wouldn't make it any easier to say. So as they arrived at Landon Farms, Jillian's fingers curled and uncurled. She worried Mariah might sense her tension, but it seemed her friend had bigger fish to fry—such as the benefit dinner.

"I can't believe Vivian Landon is sponsoring our benefit," she said as she drove in. "And that she mentioned maybe holding it at her place. Can you imagine how many people we could fit into Vivian's house? And the people she probably knows? People with money. If we raise enough, we can fund that gelding clinic I was telling you about."

Jillian just nodded. When the barn and arena came into view, she looked for Wes, thinking he might be riding. He wasn't. There was no sign of him. Not anywhere. Now that she thought about it, he hadn't called her yesterday, either. She knew his mom kept him busy exercising her colts and caring for livestock, not to mention the breeding schedule and all the other stuff a farm manager handled, but he'd found time to call the other days. But as she faced forward, she wondered if perhaps he'd gotten the message. Or if maybe he was hurt that she hadn't tried harder to get through to him.

Vivian answered the door with another wide smile, stepping through the doorway and giving Mariah a hug, her platinum-blond hair pulled into a short ponytail. The two had met at the track, Mariah had explained, and they saw each other frequently. Mariah's fiancé trained racehorses, some of them his own, some of them belonging to others. His business had taken off over the past year and Vivian liked to visit her own horses at the track.

"Look at you," Vivian said to Mariah as she moved aside so they could enter. "I've never seen your hair like that before. It's beautiful."

"I have a date with Zach tonight." Mariah seemed pleased by the praise. "We're going to celebrate the help you're giving us. Speaking of which, I really can't thank you enough." She hugged Wes's mom again, and her hands moved to the woman's shoulder as she leaned back and smiled. "You're an angel."

Vivian had the grace to appear abashed. "Nonsense." She smiled at Jillian. "I'm just glad I can help."

"Is Wes joining us?"

Hearing his name was like being jolted by a defibrillator. Jillian actually froze for a moment, but the expression on Vivian's face was all the answer she needed.

"No." The normally stress-free face looked troubled. "It was confirmed today that he's Maggie's father."

"Wow."

She'd known it was a possibility, but to hear it was actually true took her aback for some reason. It shouldn't matter one way or another, but clearly it did.

"Let's all go outside on the patio and I'll tell you about it."

The patio turned out to be a terraced backyard with a pool to the left, one of those invisible-line pools that seemed to flow into a cloudless blue sky. To the right the rocks and landscape and lush trees seemed to stretch on and on, all the way to the ocean in the distance. It took Jillian's breath away.

"Okay, I think we can meet out here." Mariah's grin was huge as she looked around. "It'll be tough, but we'll have to make it work."

Vivian laughed. Jillian marveled, forgetting for a moment about Wes's troubles. The terraces were made of granite, each a few steps down to the next level, lush foliage and blooming shrubs lining the edges. The pool blended perfectly with its surroundings. Dusky gray pebbles turned the water a darker color, the inky liquid matching the stones around the periphery. Not a leaf had fallen to dot the water's surface, not a stone looked out of place, and Jillian knew if she were to live a thousand lives, she'd never find an estate more stunning.

Wes had grown up in that pool. He'd grown up in the beautiful massive house behind her. It was one of the things she most admired about him. For all the wealth, for all the trappings, for all the things he'd no doubt been given while growing up, he was still just Wes. Still one of the nicest men she'd ever met.

Vivian had already set out a pitcher of lemonade. She poured them each a glass before sitting back and emitting a sigh.

"Does Mariah know what's going on?"

Jillian shook her head. "I didn't think it was my place to tell her."

Vivian nodded in approval. "No, but there's no keeping things under wraps now. It'll be all over the industry by month's end, mark my words. The paternity test came back. Wes is definitely the baby's father."

"Wait." Mariah glanced around the table. "Wes? A father?"

Vivian quickly filled Mariah in on the details.

"He's happy to have everything confirmed, of course, but I can tell he's a little terrified of the future." Vivian shook her head. "He's got so much on his plate right now…"

Wes's mom didn't need to explain. She made no mention of Wes's need to win a big futurity. Clearly, certain details of her son's situation she kept to herself. But Jillian knew. The pressure he had to be under could only add a new level of stress to his life, and with so much at stake…

For the first time she felt bad for not trying harder to call him back. She might refuse to fall in love with him, but she was still his friend.

Vivian changed the subject. Jillian tried to focus on

the conversation that followed, but it was difficult to offer insights on their coming fund-raiser when all she wanted to do was talk to Wes. She wouldn't be able to see him today, either, what with Mariah and her date afterward. She suddenly wished they'd arrived in separate cars.

"Are you sure?"

The tone of the question caught Jillian's attention. Mariah sounded so thrilled and grateful.

"Well, why not? It would save you from having to pay for a place to hold the event. That's half your cost right there. Wouldn't you rather have that money in the bank?"

"But the event is less than two months away."

"We can make it work," Vivian said. "Have you printed anything up advertising location?"

Mariah shook her head. "No. Not yet."

"Perfect." Vivian sat back. "We might have some trouble with the weather. It can be overcast most mornings this time of year, but it usually burns off by noon. It should be beautiful by the evening."

"I'm so excited." Mariah was all smiles. "Thank you so much—"

"Cowboy!"

They all three turned just in time to see a black-and-white blob head right for Jillian, black rear end swinging like a Ping-Pong paddle, eyes excited and what could only be a canine grin plastered on his face.

"Cowboy," she echoed, and despite her concern for Wes, she smiled. "How are you?"

"He's in trouble. I swear he heard your voice all the way down at the ranch house. I chased him all the way here."

Jillian looked into Wes's eyes and tried not to flinch. He looked like hell. Or maybe it was just the sight of him standing there, black cowboy hat, black shirt, black jeans—like a minion of the dark.

"Where's Maggie?" she asked.

Wes glanced at his mother. Jillian noted her pinched mouth. "With Maxine," Vivian answered for him.

She didn't know why that bothered her, but it did. For all they knew, Maxine might be a wonderful mother. Maybe she'd just needed some time to get her head screwed on straight.

And maybe pigs would fly.

"Oh, darn," Mariah said. "I was hoping to see her before we leave."

Wes looked as troubled as the victim of a crime. He had circles beneath his green eyes. His lips were pressed together as firmly as his mom's, too. He didn't hold her gaze for very long, either, just a quick brush of his eyes and then a smile for Mariah.

"You'll see her soon enough, I would imagine," he said.

She shouldn't have been hurt that he seemed to look right through her. She'd been the one to treat their time together as if it were no big deal. Apparently he'd gotten the message. Either that or he'd decided a one-night stand was all he wanted, too. And why did that sting?

Wes reached down and grabbed Cowboy's collar. "Sorry to disturb you."

"Don't be silly." Mariah stood and gave Wes a hug. "You'd never be disturbing us, right, Jillian?"

"No." She swallowed hard. But she couldn't look him in the eyes. The way he hardly spared her a glance made her feel ill.

"Come on, Cowboy."

And he was gone. She told herself not to watch him walk away, but she found her gaze following him anyway. Once he slipped inside the house, Cowboy shooting her one last glance over his shoulder, she turned back to her companions. They were both staring at her.

"Well?" said Mariah. "What are you waiting for?"

"Excuse me?"

Vivian shook her head, something like amused reassurance in her eyes. "He was upset when he couldn't get hold of you earlier this week."

She stared back at them. "I thought…"

"That I didn't know?" finished Vivian. "Honey, I've been around the block a time or two to know what it means when people look at each other the way you do."

That wasn't what she'd been about to say. She'd been about to confess that she'd thought she was doing them both a favor by keeping him at a distance. Only now did she admit how wrong she'd been.

"Go on," Mariah urged.

"But what about your date?"

Mariah shook her head. "Zach can wait. Go. Talk to him. I think he needs a shoulder to lean on."

She didn't refute Mariah's point. She thought so, too.

Chapter Fifteen

He couldn't get away fast enough.

"Wes, wait."

Her words were like a stab to the back. Honestly, it'd felt as though she'd stabbed him when she'd made so little effort to return his calls. It reminded him of high school all over again. Frankly, he didn't have time for her games.

"Wes," Jillian pleaded.

Cowboy stopped before he did. Releasing a sigh of impatience, he braced himself for what it would be like to look into her eyes, but nothing could prepare him for the jolt the connection sent through him—like plugging a cord into an electrical outlet.

"Sorry. Didn't hear you."

She'd caught up to him just outside his mother's house, on the granite walkway, the sun's rays touching her black hair with the reds and golds and browns of a setting sun. Her eyes swept back and forth, as if examining his features for a clue to his thoughts.

"So Maggie is really yours?"

He had to fight the urge to pull her into his arms. Stupid, irrational urge. She'd made it clear she wasn't really interested in any kind of relationship with him. To be honest, he could thank her for the favor. As it turned out, the last thing he needed was another woman in his life.

"She is."

The scent of her, berries and vanilla, wafted to him. He almost closed his eyes, caught himself at the last minute. "And are you okay with that?"

He just about bristled at the question before he reminded himself that she'd never doubted his ability to be a father. She'd asked the question because she no doubt feared the sudden thrust of fatherhood might be a tough adjustment.

"I don't really have a choice." He shook his head. "But you know that I never really worried about being a bad dad. I just want to do what's best for my daughter."

And that didn't include her mother.

"How did your meeting with Maxine go?" she asked, almost as if she read his mind.

"Fine."

She didn't need to know any more than that. He glanced down at Cowboy. The damn dog looked back and forth between the two of them as if he were following the conversation.

"Wes," she said softly, reaching out for his hand. He forced himself not to move. "I'm sorry for sort of ditching you this week."

Sort of?

He'd called her a half-dozen times and all he'd received were messages that she was busy or that she'd call him back tomorrow and that she was sorry she'd missed him. As if he were some damn dentist's office or something.

"It's fine." He eyed Cowboy again. "Come on, dog. Let's go check water."

He started to walk away, accepting that they would never be more than friends. She'd made that obvious. And that was okay. It was good. He had too much going on in his life.

She caught his hand.

He stiffened.

"No, it's not fine." She tugged him back around to face him. "I was afraid to call you. Afraid to talk to you. Afraid that I'd start to care for you more than I should."

He peered into her eyes, knew she spoke the truth, suppressed the desire to tell her it was okay. It *was* okay. Just because they'd been with each other, it didn't necessarily mean anything, not in this day and age. He should be grateful that she approached a relationship with caution.

"Maybe it was for the better." He scuffed the ground with the toe of his boot. The tip left a mark on the granite. "Life is crazy for me right now. I have Maggie, my job, competitions…"

She understood what he tried to say. He could read the disappointment in her eyes. For all her cool behavior, their time together had touched her in a way she hadn't expected, just as it had touched him.

"I see."

He swallowed against a lump of disappointment. He wanted to say to hell with it, pull her into his arms and dive in with both feet. One thing stopped him. Life.

"But, hey, you need to come out and watch me compete on Dudley next weekend."

She looked away for a moment, but when their gazes connected, she'd managed to paste a smile on her face. "I'd like that."

He could see she was sincere. "It's not you," he found himself saying.

She lifted her chin. "I know that."

"It's everything."

She nodded. "I know that, too." Her gaze skated downward again. "I feel the same way, but for different reasons."

"So we're agreed, then." He swallowed. Hard. "Friends?"

"Friends."

"Then I'll see you next weekend."

Her eyes filled with tears. Son of a bitch. The sight of those tears made him clench his fist, made him lean away from her because if he didn't do something fast, he'd give in to the instinct to tug her toward him.

"You will," she said.

They stood there, the two of them, like two empty bottles bobbing on the surface of the ocean.

"Take care, Jillian."

As a way of conveying his desire to keep things cool, the statement couldn't have been more effective. The tears in her eyes were tinged by sadness and by something that resembled disappointment, maybe even regret.

"I will." She reached for his hands and squeezed them lightly. "You, too, Wes."

SHE'D BLOWN IT. "Stupid, stupid, stupid," she muttered as she headed back inside the house.

You were smart.

How had she been smart? she all but screamed at herself. What if things had worked out with Wes? What then?

What if they hadn't?

She knew all too well what a dark pit of despair she'd

fall into if that were to happen. She should be grateful he'd cut her loose. It'd taken only one time caring just a little too much, falling just a little too hard and then being dumped, badly, for her to be afraid to fall in love. It wasn't something she cared to repeat.

"Uh-oh."

She wasn't sure who said it as she returned to Vivian's patio, but she pasted a bright smile on her face. "What?"

"My dear, you look as if you just signed the death warrant for your best friend." Vivian frowned.

Mariah's gaze connected with her own, and Jillian felt her concern. "Are you okay?"

No. She wasn't okay. She'd started to care for Wes more than she'd thought.

"He's having a tough time," Jillian said by way of explanation. "Makes me sad."

"This can't be easy for him," Mariah said.

"It's not instant fatherhood that's upset him," his mom said. "It's that woman." Vivian took a sip of her drink. "She wants to spend time with Maggie one minute, then ignore her the next, then calls him sobbing the next. It's driving him crazy."

Mariah shook her head. Jillian felt even more guilty for some reason.

"What we need to do is circle the wagons. This whole thing has the ability to affect him for the rest of his life. We can't let that happen." Vivian's eyes met hers, all but pinning her to her chair. "For that reason I will pay you to come to Wes's competition with me next weekend. We need to make sure he wins."

"You don't need to pay me." Jillian sipped her lemonade. Vivian's words had caused a lump to form in her throat. "I want him to succeed, too."

"You know how much he has riding on this?"

"I do." She tried to convey silently that she knew exactly the predicament Wes was in. "And I won't let him down."

Vivian smiled. "Good. You can ride with me to the show grounds."

THE DAY OF the competition, Jillian didn't feel very optimistic, though not about Wes's success. She knew he'd do great with or without her. She was more worried about her ability to keep her feelings bottled up inside.

She'd met with Vivian in downtown Via Del Caballo, their close-knit horse community with barns and horse pastures and cute little ranch houses as far as the eye could see. Wes hadn't called, not that she'd expected him to, but it shocked her how badly she wanted to talk to him. She'd even broken down and sent him a text message, wishing him luck this weekend and encouraging him to call her if he needed anything. He hadn't replied.

"You ready for this?" Vivian asked as they headed toward Paso Robles. "Because I have to be honest—I don't think I am."

Vivian's normally serene face seemed grooved by tension. She had lines bracketing her mouth and slight bags beneath her eyes. She was still beautiful in her caramel-colored sweater and designer jeans, but her short blond hair was mussed and her hands clenched the steering wheel of her Mercedes in a death grip.

"It'll be fine."

"I'm not so certain." Vivian peeked at her as she

made a right-hand turn. "You know how young horses are."

She did. Unpredictable at best.

"But he has to do well."

Jillian nodded, a question forming on her lips, one she'd been dying to ask Vivian for weeks. "Couldn't you, I don't know, buy a finished cutting horse and then resell it to Wes for cheap? You know, a horse that's a proven winner? With the purses being as large as they are, it wouldn't take Wes long to earn the money he needs."

But Vivian was already shaking her head. "The bulk of the Landon wealth is held in trust. I'm not the executor. My husband's brothers are."

"What?" She couldn't contain her dismay. "The uncles that tried to fight the will?"

"One and the same."

"But…" She couldn't believe it. "That's insane."

"Not as insane as it might sound. If Wes fails to earn his keep, they stand to inherit a large portion of the money." Vivian's diamond earrings sparkled in the morning light when she turned to glance at her. "It was a bone my husband threw to them when the whole inheritance mess blew up. They have everything to gain and nothing to lose by keeping a close eye on Wes's financial status."

"I've never heard of such a crazy thing."

"Crazy, but it works."

Nothing demonstrated that better than the plush vehicle they rode in. Both the interior and exterior were beige, and she wasn't certain, but she was pretty sure the seat had a heater in it—either that or she was about thirty years too early for menopause. She was lucky to make ends meet from month to month. Being self-employed didn't make things easy. She would never be able to afford a vehicle like Vivian's. Never.

"How do they know that you're not helping him?"

"An independent auditor reviews Wes's financial information on a yearly basis. We have to be very careful about how I pay him."

"Wes told me you wanted him to buy some of your yearlings."

"Yes, but at fair market value. Where he would have had the advantage was first pick. I would have made sure he'd get a winner, but he's not much for horse racing. Horse raising, as in breeding and breaking the colts, yes, but he's never been much for the sport of kings."

She knew why, too. It was a tough sport. The Landons raised quarter horses—sprinters—but it was no easier on legs and young bodies than Thoroughbred racing. Tough to watch if you had a soft heart, as Wes did. Clearly, his mother felt differently, which just went to show that despite their similarities in looks, they were different in other ways. It didn't make Vivian a bad person. Jillian had been around the sport long enough to know that some wonderful people bred horses for the track. Vivian was an example of that with her offer to help CEASE and then her suggestion that they use her house.

"It's why we only ever had one child. Don't get me wrong. We had a hell of a time conceiving Wes, but by the time he was born, there were all types of new procedures. We could have done it had we really wanted to. It just seemed…simpler this way."

She meant it would keep the infighting from happening. One child meant one heir. Easy.

"Wes tells me if he fails, most of the money will go to charity foundations."

"It will, and then some of it to his uncles. It's a convoluted mess, but I've told Wes he'll always be taken care of. I have plenty of money of my own. Money I earned for myself and that isn't part of the estate. I was an activist before I met Wes's dad. The Landon family has oil interests off the coast of California. I met him when our group tried to vandalize his office."

She couldn't be serious. But a glance at Vivian's face revealed she was. She couldn't keep her mouth from dropping open.

"What can I say? I was young and wild and free. I was also headstrong and opinionated. When I met Edward he could have had me arrested, but he didn't. Instead, he asked me out on a date and—*pfft*—I was done." She shot her a dreamy smile. "Edward encouraged me to get my degree, so I did. Spent my twenties and thirties consulting and making more money than I ever needed. Eventually, we had Wes, but it was late in life. I worried he'd grow up spoiled being an only child, but he's the joy of my life. When Edward died…"

Even in profile her face took on a look of such profound sadness it sickened Jillian's heart. It was always that way with her. She seemed to feel others' emotions far more acutely than most people.

"I'm sorry." Jillian didn't know what else to say even though the words seemed so inadequate.

"It's okay." She could tell Vivian had to force a smile. "Fortunately, Wes lives with me on the farm. He's been my rock for the past two years, which is why I hate to see him so troubled."

Yet he still kept a smile on his face. He still worked

toward his goals, still kept his head down and did what he needed to do—like this weekend's competition. He didn't let this latest nonsense with Maxine interfere with his goals. If anything, it made him more determined than ever—for Maggie's sake. She could see it in his eyes.

A woman would be lucky to have a man like that.

Chapter Sixteen

The competition was held at a private ranch, and Jillian could tell immediately that the place was every bit as much a showpiece as Landon Farms.

Surrounded by green pastures and brown wooden fences, it had a Western feel thanks to the Spanish oaks in the distance and an adobe ranch house with a terra-cotta roof. Those oaks dotted the landscape, although this time of year the leaves had just begun to sprout, the limbs casting shadows on the ground. Shelters had been painted white and brown. They matched the color scheme of a state-of-the-art metal barn the size of a small office complex. On either side of it were covered arenas. Trailers and trucks and portable stalls filled an area as big as two football fields. As they drove through the entrance marked by giant boulders, she noted the name: Rambling Rose Ranch. She saw the reason for the name as they drove toward the parking/stabling area in the back. Climbing roses covered the fences on either side of the road. She would bet it smelled fantastic in the summer, although a few obstinate blooms still clung to the vines.

"Nice place."

Coming from the woman who owned a farm that

could rival anything she'd ever seen in Kentucky, that was quite a compliment. "It is beautiful."

"Wes said he's in barn H."

Most horse competitions operated in the same manner. They always had a show office. Always row after row of single-story portable stalls, about twenty of them in a line, and all of them made out of metal frames covered by wood siding. Horses were being led, ridden, washed, groomed, clipped or readied in a host of other assorted ways, all in preparation for the competition, which looked to have already started.

"When does Wes go?"

Vivian found a spot along the fence line to park. "He told me around noon."

They had almost two hours. She glanced around, trying to spot the letters on the sides of the stalls. They'd parked by A barn. Looked as if they'd have a bit of a hike.

"He's in stall 45."

It smelled like wet earth and horses, two of her favorite things in life. The ground had been trod by hundreds of hooves, half-moon shapes stamped into the dirt. It was funny, though. As she walked toward the stalls, her stress level escalated. As Vivian had mentioned, anything could happen. What if Dudley took one look at the inside of the arena and flipped out? There was no telling what a horse would do in competition. Even the best of them freaked out, and he hadn't exactly been great the last time he'd performed in front of a crowd.

They rounded the corner, and Jillian almost ran into Vivian's back. She saw why a moment later.

"What is *she* doing here?"

There could be no doubt as to who "she" was. "Maxine," Jillian muttered.

She stood between the row of stalls, a baby stroller in front of her, and though Wes stood between them, Jillian could see enough of her face to know she wasn't pleased about something Wes had said.

"Damn," Vivian said as they set off down the long aisle.

"I'm just saying it's a bad idea," Wes was saying. "Anything could happen."

Maxine's blue eyes skated past Wes's shoulder and landed on Vivian. Jillian saw her eyes widen. Wes turned, followed Maxine's gaze. The eyes beneath the black cowboy hat rested on his mother and then her. Something changed in his expression when he spotted her, something tinged with relief and maybe even happiness. She couldn't be sure, just knew it was good to see him standing there in his blue jeans and black shirt.

"Mom, tell her that a baby stroller doesn't belong in a barn aisle."

"It doesn't."

She'd been the one who'd spoken. All eyes focused on her. She hadn't meant it to come out sounding so stern, but in for a penny, in for a pound. "A horse could kick at it. Or a horse might spook at it. Or it might tip over when a horse accidentally runs into it. Anything could happen and the only victim would be Maggie."

She saw approval in Wes's mother's eyes. Wes just seemed relieved. "That's what I told her."

Maxine looked down at the ground, and Jillian had to admit, she wasn't what she'd expected. Not at all. She reminded Jillian of those pageant girls, the kind with peroxide hair wrestled into ringlets and blue eyes outlined by too much makeup. Blonde and fake. What the hell had Wes seen in her? Then again, in the low light of a bar she might seem attractive.

And that's a catty thing to think.

She didn't care. This woman had caused Wes more trouble than he deserved. The thing was, she didn't look like a malicious bitch. The way she wouldn't look any of them in the eyes made Jillian think she was deeply uncomfortable.

"I was hoping Maggie could watch her daddy."

Jillian would have vomited if she hadn't heard the insecurity in the other woman's voice and seen what looked like wistful longing on her face. What was this?

"And she can," said Wes. "Just wheel the stroller over to the grandstands. There's plenty of room over there."

"What about after?"

"I'll meet you back here after the competition."

Was it horribly wrong of her to despise the woman on sight? This was Maggie's mother. At one point she and Wes— Well, she didn't want to think about that. She should give her a chance, especially since it was obvious she felt like a fish out of water.

"I'll walk you over there," Jillian offered even though she couldn't recall coming up with the idea. "I need to scope out where we're all going to sit, anyway."

It was as if Maxine suddenly became aware of her, as if she'd retreated so deeply inside herself she hadn't even bothered to pay attention to who had spoken earlier. She paid attention now, and she clearly thought Jillian and Wes were a couple, at least judging by the curiosity in her expression. No cattiness floated through her eyes, although Jillian couldn't imagine Maxine deemed her a threat in her black T-shirt with the logo of Natalie's farm above the left breast. Hardly dressed to party.

"Is this your girlfriend?"

Now it was Jillian's turn to stare at the ground.

"No," Wes answered.

And it stung. She turned away before Wes could see how his denial affected her, moving toward the stroller and peering down at the wide-eyed countenance of baby Maggie. When her gaze connected with her sweet green eyes, her heart just sort of went *oomph*.

"Hey there, baby girl." She leaned in close. "How's little Maggie May?" To her utter delight, the infant gurgled contentedly and then magically, she smiled. "Oh. Did you see that?" She looked up at the adults. "She just grinned at me."

"She did that for me the other day, too," Wes admitted.

"She must like you," Maxine said before peering around her. "Which way to the grandstands?"

"I'll show you." Vivian's smile was gracious for all that it was cold. It softened, though, when it shifted to Jillian. "You stay here and talk to Wes."

Wes. So tall and handsome in his black hat and black shirt. A belt buckle glittered at his waistline, the man the quintessential cowboy as he stood there staring down at her, an enigmatic look in his eyes.

"How are you?"

"Okay."

"I bet you're a nervous wreck." She forced a smile. "Where's Dudley?"

Wes pointed behind him, but then he turned quickly, calling out to Maxine and his mother. "Wait up." He strode over to where they'd stopped. "I need a good-luck kiss." She watched as he reached in and gently stroked his daughter's cheek, then bent and kissed her. The gesture made a knot of tenderness clog her throat.

He looked up, caught her staring at him. She gulped. His eyes reflected the love he felt for his little girl and something shifted inside of her, something that made her breath catch and the ground beneath her seem to roll.

She'd started to fall for him.

WES KNEW HE should be focusing on the competition, but he kept thinking about Maxine. He'd expected her to cause him grief. Instead, she'd assured him that she didn't want to get in his way. Was it crazy to hope that they could work it out?

"All right, Wes Landon, you're in next."

All that registered was his name. He looked up and noticed the gate was open and the person who'd competed before him was coming out.

Focus, Wes.

He rode a green horse, he reminded himself. The last thing he needed was to be dumped on his ass because he wasn't paying attention.

Dudley seemed far more relaxed than he was. Wes noticed the horse's lowered head and lazy ears. They were in a covered arena, one with open sides, and he'd seen horses be bothered by the lights and shadows cast by the activity along the rail. Dudley didn't even look. Once he stepped into the arena, Dudley only had eyes for the herd of cattle straight ahead. People watched from alongside the rail, some sitting in canvas chairs, some standing. Wes ignored everything as he waited for Dudley to take a misstep.

He didn't.

The point of cutting was to pull a cow out of a herd—or "cut" it—and then move the animal away from all the others. Most of the time, animals balked at being taken away from their buddies. They tried to run and duck and dart around a horse. That was the part that was scored. Dudley would be graded on how well he responded to the cow's antics and how well he kept the cow away from the herd. Some young horses lost focus the first time they were out in public, but not Dudley. He acted as if he'd been performing in front of a crowd his entire life, walking into the herd without a backward glance, ears pricked forward, body tense as he waited for Wes's commands. Compared to how he'd been at the gelding sale, it was like night and day.

"Good boy."

He'd picked an easy cow, one that wouldn't fight too hard. He wasn't here to win it. He was here to give Dudley experience. He didn't want to shatter his horse's self-confidence by picking a cow that challenged him to the point of discouragement.

"Come on, boy. Let's do this."

The cow proved to be as lazy as Wes had hoped, hardly putting up a fuss. He kept waiting for Dudley to make a mistake, maybe spook at the audience or get distracted by the other cows. He didn't, and Wes couldn't keep the grin off his face.

Perfect.

That was what it felt like when he let the cow go back to its buddies and then selected another more challenging cow. That one, too, Dudley handled like a pro. Wes's confidence grew, and so did his horse's, so much so that he let Dudley go when it came time to work their last cow. The animal didn't want to leave the comfort of the herd. It darted left. So did Dudley. It stopped dead. So did Dudley. When it suddenly took off to the right, Dudley swung around so fast he almost unseated Wes.

And he laughed.

Everything faded. His financial troubles. His fears of fatherhood. Even his concerns about Maxine. All he felt was the horse between his legs as they darted left and right, stopping and starting and moving again. When he heard the horn, he was almost sorry.

"Good job." He gave Dudley a vigorous pat.

His cheeks hurt from smiling, he realized. And his teeth felt dry. He spotted his support team right outside the arena. His mom. Maxine standing off to the side with Maggie…and Jillian. She stared at him, her grin as big as his own, excitement dancing in her eyes.

"That was incredible," she said, walking up to him, then giving Dudley a pat.

"You think?"

"I know."

She hadn't returned his calls, but he suddenly didn't care.

Chapter Seventeen

"He's going to be something else," Wes's mom said a half hour later. "Did you see him sweeping in front of that third cow? I hope they took pictures, because that was something else."

They stood outside the arena, and Jillian could tell Maxine still felt like a third wheel.

"So where do you live?"

When their gazes connected, Jillian could tell the woman was grateful to be included in a conversation. "In Santa Barbara."

"Oh, yeah?" She tried to project an air of friendliness. After all, this was the mother of Wes's child. For Maggie's sake there needed to be some peace between them. "I have clients down that way."

She saw the way Maxine tried to appear as if she were completely comfortable in her surroundings when she was anything but. At least she stood off to the side, the stroller in front of her but out of the way. More than a few horses eyed the thing with caution, but so far none of the animals had spooked. That was a good thing.

"I love it down there." And for once she smiled, and it was remarkable how much her looks improved. Jillian could see why Wes would find her attractive. "I love the coast."

Wes came toward them. Jillian was staring right at Maxine and so she saw the way she straightened up, saw the way she shyly straightened the emerald-green T-shirt she wore. Did she still have feelings for him?

"Good job," Maxine said to Wes, stepping away from the stroller, but he turned away from her, reaching in and scooping up his daughter before Maxine got too close.

"Hey there, precious." He held his daughter as tenderly as a piece of glass, nodding at his mom, who had gathered the reins of his horse.

Jillian almost felt sorry for Maxine, except she remembered what she'd done to Wes, the chaos she'd caused. Still, something made her move forward, lightly touch the woman's arm and say, "Here. I'll push the stroller back to the barn area, if you want to walk next to Wes."

And there it was again, the look of gratitude. Jillian wasn't certain what Maxine had hoped to accomplish by dumping Maggie on Wes's doorstep, but she'd begun to think the woman was just lost.

"So I guess I'll see you back at the ranch," Vivian was saying.

"I'll be leaving shortly."

"Don't forget to pick up your check."

She saw Wes smile, but it wasn't a big one. "Every little bit helps."

His mom reached up and kissed him. "You'll get there." Her eyes fell to Maggie. "You have to get there." She nudged the baby's face with her finger. "You have little Maggie to think about now." Vivian caught Maxine's eye. "Will you be bringing the baby back to the ranch?"

"I was hoping to." Maxine's gaze encompassed them all.

"Good. I think we should all have dinner."

"Oh! That would be great."

Had Vivian seen the uncertainty in Maxine's eyes? Jillian would swear some of the animosity she'd spotted on Vivian's face earlier had faded.

"Wes, why don't you and Jillian ride back together?"

Wait. *What?*

"Sure." Wes turned to her. "I just need to load up my tack in the trailer."

She glanced at Vivian, wondering what she was up to. She didn't want to ride back with Wes. She wanted to keep her distance. *Had* to keep her distance. Why was that so hard? She knew what happened when she got in too deep.

Still, she found herself asking, "Do you need help?"

"Sure."

She waved goodbye to Vivian and Maxine. Her heart began to beat harshly as she headed back to the barn.

"Are you going to come and watch me ride in the futurity, too?"

Her throat was so dry it was all she could do to croak, "Of course."

"I hope he's as quiet there as he was here."

She knew she had to tell him. "He likes competing."

"It sure seems that way."

She stopped. Wes did, too, Dudley's ears pricking forward as if curious what they were doing. She closed her eyes and silently told the horse to be patient.

"He likes performing in front of an audience."

"You think so."

"I *know* so."

"How?" He glanced at his horse. "I mean, what signs do you look for to make you think that?"

She swallowed. Here it was, the moment she'd been waiting for. The moment she'd known was coming when she'd woken up next to him. "No signs." She lifted her chin. "He told me he likes it."

"Told you?"

She reached into her back pocket, fished out one of the business cards she always carried with her. "Read this."

He glanced at the card. "I don't need this. I know who you are."

"Read what it says."

His confusion was evident, but he did as she asked. "'Jillian Thacker, animal communicator.'" Their gazes connected. "Animal communicator?"

Her heart had taken off like the horses his mom raced. "I can talk to them, Wes."

"Talk to *who*?"

"Animals."

His eyes widened so quickly it would have been comical if this hadn't been Wes standing in front of her, if she hadn't seen the exact same look on other faces throughout her life. If that look didn't usually come from men…right before they laughed or called her crazy or flat-out refused to believe her.

"Talk."

She nodded.

"As in actually converse with them?"

"Not exactly. They shoot me images, pictures of what's in their minds, like a TV screen. For instance, when Dudley came out of the arena, I asked if he was happy and he shot me pictures of the audience. I interpreted that to mean he liked being watched."

Wes took off his cowboy hat and ran his fingers through his hair. Dudley nudged him, almost as if silently trying to reassure him what she said was true, but she could tell by the look in Wes's eyes that he wasn't sure what to think.

"That's crazy." She heard him mutter.

Of course it was. That was what people always thought. Well, okay, not everyone. Occasionally she'd meet someone who believed in her gifts, instantly believed, but those people were few and far between.

"I know it sounds completely incredible, but just think about it, Wes. I've been helpful to you, haven't I? When you were having trouble with that lead, I told you it was because Dudley was sore. I knew that because of my gift, although I didn't know if he had bone pain or muscle pain. I just knew something was up, and I was right, wasn't I?"

He peered down at her intently, and she could see it happening, see him fight it. He didn't want to believe her. No. That wasn't it. He could believe her if he wanted to; he just didn't possess the faith it took to believe in things you couldn't see.

Such a disappointment.

She'd known it was possible, had hoped that because he was a horse person it might be different, but she should have known better. At least when Jason had broken up with her, it hadn't been because of her gifts. He'd simply cheated on her—not that it made any difference. Loss was loss, and for her, because of her abilities, that loss hurt twenty times worse than it did for a normal person. At least, that was what she'd reasoned out over the years.

"You have been helpful." She heard him say. "I just have a hard time believing it's because of secret signals or invisible voodoo."

Why wasn't she surprised?

"But I guess it doesn't matter." She saw him take a deep breath, saw him force a smile. "You're good with horses. I can't deny that." He moved closer. "I missed you this week."

She stepped back. It mattered to her, damn it. She hadn't realized exactly how much until that moment when she felt the breath slide out of her. She wanted him to believe. In her. In her gifts.

Maybe you can bring him around.

Maybe she could, and maybe she couldn't, and if it didn't work out, what then? More crushing disappointment? More horrible days and long nights mourning the loss of yet another lover. No thanks. She'd been right to pull back from him. It'd been smart to keep him at a distance. She just hadn't expected it to hurt so much.

"I've missed you, too, Wes. Missed talking to my friend."

She hadn't meant to put the emphasis on that last word, but perhaps it was for the best. He'd received the message loud and clear.

"I see."

She could tell her stepping back from him had stung, could tell he wasn't happy, could tell she'd wounded him.

"It's not you." She looked down at the ground for a moment, trying to sort through her thoughts. "It's me." She had to take a deep breath before she could look him in the eyes. "I'm not like a normal person. I feel things. Deeply. Too deeply. Before I met you, I'd decided to never get into a relationship again."

"That's stupid."

"Not for me, it's not." She lifted her head. "You might not believe in my gifts, but I know what I feel. I know what I see, too. But most of all, I know what it does to me when a relationship goes south. I won't let that happen with us."

She expected him to get angry, maybe even to argue with her, but he'd never been one to force his will on others, not with horses, not with his dog and clearly not with people, either.

"Goodbye, Wes." She reached up on tiptoe and kissed his cheek. "I'll catch a ride home with your mom after all."

She turned away before she could change her mind or before she did something stupid…like tell him that walking away from him was one of the hardest things she'd ever had to do.

Chapter Eighteen

Damn it.

What the hell had happened? One minute she was congratulating him on a good ride and the next she was breaking up with him.

He banged his steering wheel with his fist.

His mood didn't improve any when he learned Maxine's parents had accepted his mom's invitation to dinner. Great. The last thing he felt like doing was socializing. He'd met them once before when he'd gone over to their house to pick up Maggie, and they'd made it clear they thought he'd somehow done their daughter wrong. Nothing could be further from the truth, something he worked to set straight the moment they were all seated in his mom's family room, Maggie held in his mother's arms.

"Look," he said. "I want you two to know that I had no idea Maxine was pregnant. Granted, she tried to call me, and I never called her back, but at no time did she tell me she was carrying my child."

It might have been a blunt thing to say, especially since they'd all just sat down, but he'd needed to get things out in the open.

They were an older couple. Tom's gray hair was thinning in the shape of a U, and Dianne sported shoulder-length brown hair. They both shot their daughter a look.

"Is this true, Maxine?" Dianne asked.

It seemed Maxine hadn't expected the truth to come out, at least not right away. "Yes."

"For the love of God, Max, why didn't you tell him?"

Maxine wouldn't look anyone in the eye, and for the first time Wes wondered if she'd simply been overwhelmed by it all.

"I wasn't sure it was his," Maxine finally answered.

Her dad sank back on the couch. Dianne's cheeks filled with color, as if she was embarrassed.

"I thought it would be best to wait and see." She glanced at her daughter. "And then afterward I thought maybe it would be better to just give Maggie over to him to be raised."

"Dear Lord," Dianne said. She met Wes's eyes. "It appears I owe you an apology."

He lifted a hand. "No, no. It's all right."

"No, we do." She glanced at her husband. "We haven't been very friendly toward you, because we thought you dumped our daughter when she got pregnant."

"Wes would never do something like that," Vivian interjected.

"I see that now," Tom said, holding out his hand toward Wes.

From that point forward, Tom and Dianne were remarkably nice. They were clearly disappointed with their daughter, and Wes suspected there would be words later, but at least they seemed to accept that he wasn't some kind of irresponsible dilettante.

"Thanks for coming to my defense," Wes whispered

to his mother as he scraped the remains of his dinner off his plate and into a garbage compactor. Cowboy whined softly, as if reminding Wes that he didn't need to waste all that good food. "Not a chance, buddy," he told the dog.

"Are you kidding?" his mom said, rinsing off a plate and sticking it in the dishwasher. She could have easily afforded a maid, but his mom wasn't that type, something Wes had always admired about her. "It was all I could do not to throttle that woman when I realized what she'd allowed her parents to think," she added.

"Me, too." He handed his mom a plate. "I need to talk to her, though. We need to sort out how we're going to work all this out." He rested his hands on the counter. So much chaos in his life. Maybe it was for the best that Jillian didn't want to see him anymore.

"Poor baby."

The comment made him look up.

His mom stared at him sympathetically. "You're under a lot of pressure."

"That's an understatement."

She held his gaze through a veil of steam that rose up from the tap water. The sound of the running tap ensured their words wouldn't be overheard. "What happened between you and Jillian?"

The plate he'd been holding clattered to the counter. They both reached for it at the same time.

"Everything all right in there?" Dianne called.

"Fine," his mom called back, but she still stared at him in question, though she'd managed to rescue the plate from his clumsy fingers.

"Clearly, something did because she practically threw herself into my car."

He didn't really want to talk about it. Not now. Maybe not ever.

"Nothing happened," he hedged. "She just changed her mind about riding home with me."

His mom shut off the water and turned to face him. "Wesley Landon, don't try to brush my question off."

"I don't want to talk about it."

"I know the two of you were intimate."

It was crazy that his cheeks could still turn bright red. "Mom!"

"I'm not a fool. And I was happy for you. The two of you are perfect for each other."

He shook his head. "She talks to animals."

"I know."

"You know?"

"Mariah told me weeks ago."

"Why didn't you tell me?"

His mom snorted. "Why? When I know you don't believe in that kind of thing?"

He opened his mouth only to clap it closed again. She was right.

"Did you call her a quack?"

"Of course not," he replied loudly.

"So what happened?"

Wes almost forced her to drop the topic, but something made him consider the question. Aside from Zach, his mom was his closest friend. If he couldn't confide in her, there was nobody he could talk to right away... and suddenly he wanted to talk.

"She's afraid."

His mom snorted. "Who isn't?"

"She mentioned being different. Said she feels things

more deeply than a normal person—whatever that means."

"Why don't you ask her?"

"Because she made it clear she didn't want to see me anymore."

"And you let her walk away."

"I had no choice."

"Son, you always have a choice."

He was taller than his mom. A lot taller. In that moment he wished he were a little boy again, one without all the fears of an adult.

"Trust your heart, honey."

"It's not my heart that's the problem."

His mom's eyes widened almost imperceptibly. "No?"

He realized then just how much he cared for Jillian. "No."

She pulled him in tight, but only for a moment, because she stepped back and slapped him on the arm. "Talk to Jillian. But first settle things between you and Maxine. Take her out on the back porch. I have a feeling things will be a lot clearer once you two get things ironed out."

He hoped so. Lord, how he hoped so.

"I'll send her out to you."

He nodded, but he'd have been lying if he said he wasn't nervous as he waited by the pool. His mom had turned on the lights. Lawn sconces cast a pearlescent glow over the granite landscape.

"Wow. This is the life."

He hadn't even heard her slip through the door. Not surprising. He'd been so deep in thought—thinking about Jillian and her "gifts"—that he probably wouldn't have heard a 747 landing.

"My mom has good taste."

"She's nice, too."

Funny, it was the first time he noticed what Maxine had worn. A flimsy sundress that would have been more appropriate at a pool party than a dinner. She looked cold, not surprisingly. It was the end of February, and this close to the ocean it could get chilly fast.

"Do you need a jacket or something?"

"No. I'm fine."

She looked pretty standing there by the pool. It reminded him of the first night they'd met. They'd both been a little tipsy and she'd been completely charming, and if he were honest with himself, he'd been looking for some company. The night of the Turf Club dinner had been tough to bear without his dad. It'd been the first time they'd been to a trackside function without him, and if it had been hard on him, it had been even harder on his mom. He'd been searching for a way to escape and he'd found it in Maxine's arms.

"That first night we met, you were hoping to net a big fish, weren't you?"

A quick glance revealed her mouth opening and closing a few times before she said, "I beg your pardon?"

"You were thinking I was some rich racehorse owner living off his family's money."

He saw her look away, embarrassed.

"It's okay. You don't need to answer. I know you hooked up with Kanal Khuruna the same week you went home with me."

"How do you know that?"

"Small world, plus Kanal told me. I didn't believe him at first, but I do now, especially after you admitted you didn't know who the baby's father was until you saw her eyes."

They weren't dark brown. Maggie's skin was fair. Maxine hadn't needed a DNA test to know he was the father.

"I'm sorry, Wes. Sorry about everything."

Funny, but he believed her. "I don't have a lot of money."

She lifted her chin up and he could tell she was insulted. "This isn't about about money. I was scared. Terrified, really. I never planned to get pregnant. Sure, I was hoping to meet someone nice that night, but I really wasn't trying to snag a rich guy."

"I still wish you'd told me you were pregnant."

"I would have if you'd called me back."

"I thought you were calling to hook up again."

"As if. You'd made it clear you wanted nothing to do with me."

"You make me sound like a jerk."

"You were being a jerk."

"Not when you consider I thought you were with Kanal and that all you were after was money."

"You still could have called me back."

He gulped back his anger. She had a point. Damn it.

"Look, it's all water under the bridge right now. Let's just focus on the future, okay?"

He saw her take a few deep breaths herself. "Fine. How do you want to work this?"

"I'm hoping you'll give Maggie to me and my mom to raise. Your parents are older. I can't imagine them wanting to raise another child, but I don't know—maybe I'm wrong, maybe I'm not. I just know this is a good place to raise a kid. I was happy here growing up. I'm sure Maggie will be, too."

She licked her lips. He knew she contemplated her options. Knew she was weighing out the pros and cons of being footloose and fancy-free, of saddling him with the burden of a child, not that Maggie would ever be a burden to him.

"I'll think about it."

It was more than he'd hoped for, and the relief he felt was instantaneous. "Okay, good."

He motioned toward the house. "You look like you're freezing. We should probably get back inside."

She didn't say another word. He didn't, either. He was too busy thinking about how much his life had changed, and how he somehow knew what Maxine's decision would be.

Cowboy greeted him when he slipped back inside. He bent down to scratch the dog's black-and-white head. "Maybe I'm the psychic now, Cowboy."

Jillian.

His heart began to beat a little faster. His mom was right. He needed to trust his heart. She might have told him goodbye today, but he wasn't ready to let her go.

Chapter Nineteen

Mariah filled her in on the big happenings up at the house.

"I guess Maxine finally came to her senses. She's giving full custody of Maggie to Wes."

Jillian couldn't believe it. "What happened to change her mind?"

Mariah's red hair, always a handful, seemed extra curly this morning. Not surprising since they were out of doors watching Natalie work her new horse in one of her outdoor arenas—the only one that wasn't full of jumps. Her blond friend rode in a Western saddle, something that a year ago Jillian never would have expected to see, not in this lifetime, at least. Natalie galloped around at a breakneck speed, hair flying, only to pull the horse up in the middle of the arena.

"Oh, that was great," Mariah called.

"I think it was, too," Natalie called back. "But I wish I knew what the hell I was doing."

"Wes says he knows someone who could help you."

"Does he?" Natalie patted the dark bay gelding that she'd purchased at the bull-and-gelding sale. "I would love to have someone work with me from the ground."

She went back to working the horse, and Mariah

turned back to Jillian. "So what are you wearing next week?"

"Clothes," Jillian answered.

"Ha-ha. Very funny." Mariah shook her head. "I hope you have something spectacular picked out. There's bound to be some good-looking men there, although I'm bummed things didn't work out between you and Wes. He really is a good guy."

The statement brought to mind images of Wes staring into Maggie's eyes. Of the way he scratched Cowboy behind the ears. Of the love in his eyes when he spoke to his mother. Yes. A good man indeed.

"If you need help picking something out, let me know."

"No, I'm good." She had something already.

But on the day of the big benefit dinner, she suddenly found herself panicking about what to wear. Everyone who was anyone would be at the event. It was important that she look her best. That was what she told herself. Certainly it wasn't that she'd be seeing Wes for the first time since she'd told him goodbye. That had nothing to do with it at all.

The gates to Landon Farms were wide-open. She had arrived early to help Mariah and the other CEASE members set up for the event. Fortunately, the weather had cooperated. Most of the guests would be out on the back patio and it looked as if that would be beneath starry skies. Still, as the valley opened up before her, she couldn't help but look to the right and the barn and Wes's home. Couldn't help but wonder where he was and what he was doing.

"There you are," Mariah said when she entered the house. "Wow. Don't you look like a million bucks?"

"A million bucks is what we're hoping to raise," she said as she hugged her friend.

"Yeah, well, in that red dress someone might just offer to pay that to spend a night with you."

"Mariah!"

Her friend laughed and as she stepped back, Jillian glanced around for Wes. She didn't see him. Told herself that was good. She didn't need to see him.

"He's down at the house with Maggie. He'll be up later, once the babysitter arrives."

"Oh, no. I was just looking to see how the flowers were coming."

Mariah gave her a look of bemused reproach. "Yeah, right."

The next hour passed so quickly she didn't have time to think about Wes. Well, that wasn't precisely true. She thought about him as she set out flowers in rooms that had pictures of Wes as a child standing in the winner's circle with one of his mom's racehorses. Wes as a young boy showing a steer at some kind of event, probably the local fair. Wes standing next to his mom in a cap and gown. So handsome. So much like his father, she noticed.

"He was a charmer, that one."

She almost dropped the photo of Wes and his father. "Vivian." She turned to face their hostess. "I didn't see you there." She glanced with chagrin toward the picture. "I'm sorry. I probably shouldn't be touching your things."

"Don't be ridiculous. I suspect everyone will be in and out of this room tonight."

They stood in a formal living room, one with a massive fireplace set into the middle of a wall and views of the ocean off the back. Someone had lit a fire. Its warmth tickled her legs.

"You look lovely," Vivian said.

Her hand went to her throat, though she wore no jewelry. The halter-top dress was a little more revealing than she remembered from the store and to say she was a bit self-conscious would be an understatement.

"Thanks. You do, too."

Vivian smiled. "Actually, I'm glad I caught you. I've been wanting to talk to you."

She didn't want to talk. She just wanted to get through the night because standing there looking at the photos of Wes had done something to her. Such a knot of emotion clogged her throat. It made her hands tremble and her legs shake.

"Sit," Vivian ordered, patting the couch next to her.

Jillian felt like Cowboy, but she grudgingly did as ordered. She was completely on edge as she did it, though, worried that her dress might gap open or that Vivian would find fault with the mascara she'd used or her choice in strappy high heels.

It's just Vivian.

The nicest woman Jillian had ever met. A woman who had one of the biggest hearts in the world. Just look at how she was helping them with CEASE—

"Why are you doing this to yourself?"

She looked up sharply into Vivian's eyes. "Doing what?" she asked.

"Telling yourself you're not in love with my son."

She gasped.

"You are in love with him, aren't you?"

No. She wasn't.

Her gaze caught on the framed picture on the mantel

and from nowhere came a groan. She closed her eyes, shook her head, felt her fingers clutch the edge of the couch as if she might fall off it if she didn't hold on tight.

"That's what I thought."

No. She wasn't. She flatly refused to believe it. She'd made sure she wouldn't. Had made sure to keep him at a distance after their one time together. She'd kept him at arm's length and then he'd done the same and so it wasn't true.

Vivian clasped her hands and squeezed. "Wes tells me you're afraid of falling in love."

She almost laughed. "Afraid would be an understatement. More like…terrified."

Vivian's eyes were a haunting, piercing green. "Why?"

How to tell this woman, how to explain to this wonderful, kind woman, that she'd lost so many things in her life. That grief didn't affect her like a normal person. It stung with the sharp lash of a laser. It gouged her heart out. It brought her so low that there were times when she had wished…

She hated remembering those moments. It made her ashamed. She had such an amazing gift. A God-given one. She should be grateful for her life, not sad that she'd been left behind.

"You've lost quite a few loved ones, haven't you?"

"Yes."

"It hurts when they're gone." Vivian looked away, her gaze growing unfocused. "When I married Wes's father, I was so terribly in love. I thought we'd live our whole lives together. That we'd both grow old. We'd both get gray and lose our teeth and live long enough to see Wes

grow up and have children of his own. I have that now."
She patted Jillian's hand. "But I don't have Edward."

The sadness in Vivian's eyes made Jillian's own eyes
warm with tears. She had loved Wes's father deeply.
That much couldn't be doubted.

"But you know what, dear Jillian?" She shook her
head. "I wouldn't trade one day of my life with him.
Granted, the loss of him was terrible. Horrible. Gone
too soon thanks to a faulty tire and a wet road. Ridiculous, really, when you think about all the stupid
things you do when you're young, and then you're driving down the road and that's…it." The hand went back
to squeezing hers. "But I loved him. And I wouldn't
change a thing about our lives together. The pain of
his loss haunts me every day, but I have the memory
of our love to hold on to, as well. And Wes. Without
that love there wouldn't be a Wes or a Maggie, and to
not have those two wonderful, lovely human beings in
the world, well, that would have been an even greater
tragedy, don't you think?"

Something hot fell on her cheek. Tears. She knew
what the woman was trying to say, knew what she was
encouraging her to do.

"There." Vivian straightened the skirt of her silk
dress, the color of it the same as her eyes. "I've said
what I wanted to say." She leaned in and kissed Jillian
on the cheek. "Good luck, my dear."

HE'D TOLD HIMSELF he was prepared to see her. He'd
been wrong.

She stood by the side of the pool, beneath a cloudless, starry sky, a propane heater—the kind shaped like
a mushroom—casting a mercury glow over her ink-

black hair. She was talking to someone. A male some-one. He couldn't hear what they were saying, because music played in the background. People even danced near one side of the pool. And it amazed him, really, just how instantly his hackles rose at the sight of her standing there with that man. They weren't a couple. They would never be a couple. She'd made that clear.

She looked past the man's shoulder and met his gaze. He saw her stiffen slightly, noticed that she couldn't hold his gaze for very long, and wondered if she felt it, too: the kick to the gut. The tendril of electricity that seemed to stretch between them.

He moved toward her.

"...so you really talk to them, then?" the man was saying. "Talk as in you and I are talking."

"No," Wes interrupted. "She doesn't actually talk to them. She flashes images at them and they flash her back. Like a big-screen TV." Or at least that's how his mom had explained it.

The man—whoever he was—turned halfway to see who'd spoken.

Wes bent and kissed Jillian's cheek. It wasn't meant to be a stamp of ownership. It was meant to be the im-personal peck of a good friend, but he let his lips lin-ger a bit too long—couldn't help himself, because as he leaned closer, he smelled her again and he'd always loved berries and vanilla.

"Wes." He heard her say, startled.

He drew back and smiled. "I've been looking for you all night," he admitted.

She glanced at her companion, then back at him, looking nervous. "Jim, this is Wesley Landon."

"Landon of Landon Farms?" Wes nodded. Jim reached out to shake his hand. "Pleasure to meet you."

Wes couldn't stop himself from looking back at Jillian. In her red dress and strappy matching sandals she looked more beautiful than ever. She'd put her hair up, had somehow piled the short locks atop her head. Regal and elegant and so damn sexy with those long legs peeking out from beneath the knee-high hem of her dress that all he wanted to do was drag her back to his place.

"How's Maggie?" she asked in a transparent attempt to change the subject.

"Asleep upstairs." He smiled at Jim. "I have an infant daughter."

He saw Jim's gaze dart to his ring finger, as if he was trying to figure out if he were married. More like hoping he was married. Wes almost smiled.

"Good for you," Jim said.

"My mom was afraid to leave her down at my place with a teenage babysitter. She's protective that way."

Jillian smiled, too. "Your daughter's a lucky little girl."

"Yes, she is."

A new song came on over the speakers. Wes didn't give himself time to think—he just grabbed her hand. "Dance with me."

"Oh, but I—"

"No buts." He winked at Jim. "Nice meeting you." He tugged Jillian toward the spot where couples danced.

"That was rude."

"No," he said, spinning her around to face him near the other couples. "What was rude was the way you told me to get lost last week."

"I did not."

He held her too closely, and as it always did when he touched her, the electricity that stretched between them danced along his arms and his belly. It'd been weeks since they'd slept together, and yet he still craved her just as badly as that first time.

"You did, and you've been avoiding me this week." He felt her tense in his arms. "My mom says she's asked you to come over at least a half a dozen times."

"I've been busy."

"You've been avoiding me," he repeated.

Just as quickly as it'd come, the tension left her body. "All right, I have."

That a girl. It was one of the things he loved about her. She didn't mince words, always told the truth, even when that truth reflected badly upon her.

"I just thought it would be—" she shrugged "—easier."

"Easier, yes. Change things, no."

She leaned back, stared into his eyes, and it was all Wes could do not to drop down and kiss her. Right there in front of God and everyone.

"Wes, please."

"Please what?"

"Don't."

"My mom says you're in love with me."

She gasped.

"I told her she was wrong, but now…" His gaze swept her up and down as he danced her toward a darker part of the terrace. "After seeing how you dressed up for me. After watching the way your eyes lit up when you spotted me—"

"Don't flatter yourself."

"They did, and that's okay, because I lit up inside when I saw you, too."

Her mouth dropped open. Green eyes widened.

"You might be too scared to take it any further, but I'm not."

He bent and did what he'd been wanting to do since the moment he'd seen her standing there in that damn dress, that damn silk dress that wasn't much of a barrier against his own white button-down and jeans. She resisted at first, but not for long. As if suddenly calling surrender, her mouth opened beneath his own. He groaned. She did, too, as their tongues found each other, entwined. Her hips brushed against his and the contact was fire. He had to come up for air because he knew if he didn't, he would lift the skirt of her dress and open his jeans—

"Come on."

"Wes, no."

"You're going to prove it to me tonight."

"Prove what?"

"That you don't love me. That this is all carnal. That it's just sexual attraction and that it'll go away."

"We can't do that."

"Why not?"

"Because I do care for you, Wes, and if we sleep together, I don't know if I'll have the strength to walk away this time."

His world tipped again, but this time for a different reason—this time it was because of the absolute finality in her gaze.

"Why are you so afraid?"

She shook her head. "Your mom asked me the same question. I couldn't explain it to her, either." And she sounded so torn, so genuinely distressed, that Wes's heart broke. "It just hurts too much when it all goes away."

"But it won't go away, Jillian. I promise you that."

"Nothing last forever, Wes. Look at your mom and dad."

He winced.

"Look at *my* mom and dad." She wiped at her eyes, and he realized she cried. "I'm sorry." She took a step back. "I'm so sorry. I tried to make that clear to you last week. I haven't changed my mind—instead, I think I'm even more determined." She started walking backward, and even though it was dark, he could see the sadness in her eyes. "Stay away from me, Wes. I'm bad news."

Chapter Twenty

She was the worst sort of pond scum. The lowest form of fungus. The nasty green stuff that grew on stale water. Wait. That was algae. Whatever.

As Jillian drove home, she wiped her eyes. She probably shouldn't be driving. And Mariah would be mad. She'd bailed on the party. But she couldn't stay. She just couldn't be near Wes.

If you love him so much, what in God's name are you doing dumping him?

Because she would never be married, have kids, be a wife. Deep down inside, she'd always known that. If they got hurt, their pain would become hers. If they became sick, she would be sick with fear. If they died... Well, she couldn't even think about that. So the solution was to be alone, and it wouldn't be so bad. She had her animals. Well, not her animals, everyone else's pets, but her fear of losing that connection to a person she loved, the constant worry, it was why she preferred to be alone. Why she refused to have anything in her life that she might have to watch walk away—or worse.

She heard from Mariah that the fund-raiser was a rousing success. Between ticket sales and the silent auction they raised nearly $10,000. It was a boon they'd use to fund Mariah's efforts to hold a free gelding clinic.

She kept tabs on Wes and his daughter through Mariah. Apparently, Maxine had been true to her word, allowing Wes full custody of his little girl. She couldn't be happier for him. The only thing that remained was to win the cutting horse competition—a tall order after all the reading she'd been doing on the event. The Million Dollar Futurity was one of the Cutting Horse Association's premier events, a showcase of talent geared toward newcomers in the industry. She'd looked at the entries online and learned that Wes had entered Dudley in the main event. An open class for both professionals and amateurs alike. The purse wasn't actually a million dollars. It was split between the winners with first place getting the bulk. She didn't know how much Wes needed to win to meet his goal. She knew he had to do well. The event would be streamed live over the internet and she planned to watch.

"No, you're not," Mariah told her when she explained her plans. They were sitting in Jillian's kitchen, her friend having insisted she come over to cheer her up, although so far it wasn't working. "You're going with us to watch."

"No, Mariah. Seriously. I can't." The mere thought of it made her feel queasy. "He probably hates me, Mariah, and I don't blame him. I'm such a coward. I couldn't possibly show up at his cutting competition."

"You'll show up and you'll do your thing, too." Mariah waved her fingers. "Vivian is counting on you."

Vivian. She missed Wes's mother. A more down-to-earth woman she'd never met. Kind. Sweet. Genuinely concerned for her son's happiness.

"Surely Vivian doesn't want me around any more than Wes."

"Are you kidding? She's convinced you're their secret weapon."

Secret weapon. Hardly. More like distraction. "I still don't think it's a good idea."

"You're leaving with us tonight and that's that. We're all staying at a hotel, you included. The competition starts at the crack of dawn and so we have to leave tonight in order to watch his go."

She knew when the competition started. She'd planned to get up early. Had cleared her day just so she could watch nonstop.

"Mariah—"

Her friend got up from the kitchen table. "Be ready to leave by five. It'll take four hours to get there. We'll pick up dinner on the way out of town. Fast food."

"I'm not going."

"Yes, you are."

"Mariah—"

"Be ready by five."

She wouldn't be ready. She wouldn't even be home. She'd leave. Hide out someplace because she knew if she saw Wes again...

Coward.

She couldn't avoid him forever. She would see him at Mariah and Zach's wedding. Would she hide out there, too? And if there was a chance she could help, if she could help to soothe Dudley, shouldn't she do it?

Damn it.

So it was that she found herself at the one place she didn't want to be the next morning—an equestrian multiplex just outside of Sacramento.

"I've never been to a cutting horse competition," Zach, Mariah's future husband, said as they slipped out of Mariah's truck. "This will be a first for me."

"You fit right in," Mariah said as she came around the truck and stood up on tiptoe to kiss his cheek, but afterward she tweaked the black cowboy hat he wore, and the gesture, as well as the look they exchanged, made Jillian turn away. She was happy for her friend. Overjoyed that despite their different backgrounds, she and her dark-haired, blue-eyed Zach had found their happily-ever-after.

You might have had one, too.

Maybe, but it was too late now, and she refused to dwell on it. Instead, she studied their surroundings. It was the first time she'd ever been to one of the big cutting horse competitions, but it reminded her of the big hunter shows—without the over-the-top stall decorations. The horses all wore Western saddles, too, and this early in the morning their breath jetted out like twin streams of steam as they galloped around a covered arena. The place they were at seemed to have half a dozen of them. Jillian had no idea how Mariah knew where they were going, but luckily, she seemed to have a good idea of where Wes was hiding out.

"Maybe I should head straight for the main arena. Find a spot for us."

They had just come around to yet another arena and there was no mistaking the sight of Vivian standing by the rail, a stroller out in front of her.

"I didn't eat very much at breakfast. Maybe I can get something on the way. I smell food."

"You—" Mariah hooked an arm through her own

"—are not going anywhere. You need to take a look at Dudley. Tell us how he's feeling."

It was too late. Vivian had spotted them. "You made it," she called out.

Jillian told herself not to glance inside the arena. Told herself, but she did it anyway. She recognized Dudley right away. It startled her seeing the little horse for the first time in a long while. He'd gained weight. And muscle. His head didn't seem so big for his body anymore, and his tail and mane had caught the early-morning light; it turned the red strands gold. She didn't look at Wes. She couldn't. It was too painful.

You could end that pain if you weren't such a coward.

Yes, end the pain now, she told that voice, but for how long? With her track record, not very.

"He looks great," Mariah said, her eyes on the sorrel gelding, too. "I can't believe how much he's improved."

"Zach, so good to see you." Vivian smiled at Mariah's fiancé, but that smile slipped a bit when she saw Jillian. "I didn't know you were coming."

Jillian glanced at Mariah quickly. Mariah had the grace to blush, something that was instantly noticeable with her fair skin and pink cheeks.

"I thought I could help." She would kill Mariah. "With Dudley, I mean."

At last she dared to look into Vivian's eyes. She expected anger, disappointment and, most of all, disapproval. What she saw instead was sadness, patience and understanding. A lump lodged itself in her throat.

"Of course you can help."

It took her breath away, Vivian's kindness. She should have expected it. Wes had learned patience and understanding from someone, clearly his mom.

"Wes," Vivian called. "Look who's here."

He'd been so busy working Dudley he hadn't even noticed them standing by the rail. She waited for their gazes to connect, chickened out at the last moment and decided to peer into the stroller instead. Because it was so early, they had Maggie bundled up like a burrito, but she'd grown wisps of dark hair since the last time she'd seen her. She wore a pink hat and she obviously slept, but she couldn't have looked more like a doll if she'd tried.

"Precious," she whispered.

When she looked up, Wes had stopped by the rail, and his eyes weren't filled with hatred or loathing or even surprise. They were filled with what could only be called delight.

"They got you to come."

They. She glanced at Mariah and Wes. So that was why her friend had been so insistent. Surely she could have told her Wes wanted her there.

"They said you needed me."

"I do." He patted Dudley. "You're the reason we're here. I didn't want you to miss it."

Her ribs seemed to shrink as her heart began to swell. The Landons would be the death of her. They would kill her with kindness.

"Thanks."

She had to force her gaze away, but the image of him was etched into her mind. Beige cowboy hat, mint-green long-sleeved shirt, dark brown chaps over his denim jeans.

"So what does he tell you?" Wes asked.

It wasn't so much what the horse told her as it was the

look in his eyes and the way he stood there alongside the rail, ears pricked forward, nostrils flaring.

"He's ready." —

HE TOLD HIMSELF to keep calm. Strangely, seeing Jillian had done exactly that—calmed him. She was his talisman. His good-luck charm. And he needed her...in more ways than one. She might keep chickening out on him, but he would change her mind. Maybe. Eventually.

Don't think of that now.

What he needed to do was focus. He was seventh in the go, which meant fresh cattle. That could be good, that could be bad. It also meant an early score. Sometimes judges tended to hold back a bit in expectation of the better horses that would compete later in the day. Then again, going early could work in his favor. Sometimes if a horse was truly spectacular, they would score them well to ensure they stayed on the leaderboard, sometimes too well. One never knew which way the wind would blow.

All too quickly they called him to the staging area. The back-gate people could be fierce about making sure people were ready to go when their turn came. He would need to sit at that gate and wait, the worst part of the whole competition, standing there, his horse sensing the coming activity, his own body growing more and more tense.

"Good luck," his mom called.

He was waved off by his support group, and his mom headed to the spectator area at one end of the arena. There was even a bar in the upstairs portion of the facility. Frankly, he wished he could run up the step and choke down a shot of whiskey. Instead, he headed toward the waiting area.

The arena was state-of-the-art. It was climate controlled, and riders entering via a narrow pathway that allowed a minimal amount of heat or cold to enter the building. At one of the short ends, the one to his left, a raised viewing area afforded spectators an unobstructed view of the riders in the arena. Actually, it resembled more of a restaurant with a snack bar and round tables and comfy chairs. The place was packed. As was the grandstand seating to his right. The judges were opposite the spectators, on a raised dais, their cowboy hats and neutral-colored pants and long trench coats the standard uniform for people in their position.

"Wes Landon, you here?" the gate person called.

Wes acknowledged his arrival, his palms beginning to sweat. Dudley, as if sensing his escalating tension, tossed his head.

"There's three in front of you."

He probably should have arrived earlier. Should have been there for the first couple of goes to watch the herd. He did his best to make up for lost time, tracking which cows looked slow, which cows seemed to be fast and which cows were too full of themselves. This was a fresh herd. Nobody on the show grounds had any idea how they would cut. That was one of the major drawbacks of going early. He wouldn't have an hour to study which cows would give him the best run for his money.

"You ready?" the gate person asked, a younger cowboy with a felt hat that matched his own.

"Ready as I'll ever be."

The last rider had had a good go. He nodded to the cowboy as the gate swung open. The scores were announced over the loudspeaker, though they lagged behind by one or two riders—most of the time—but Wes would be surprised if the guy didn't mark a high score.

His head began to pound. He rolled his shoulders, and Dudley's head lifted as he nudged him forward. This was it. Make-it-or-break-it time. He had no idea how many entries there were. No idea how much first place would actually pay out at the end of the day. All he knew was that he had to mark a high score.

"Let's do it, Dudley."

His horse knew the game. Most of the time, he worked Dudley in a dry arena—meaning no cattle—so the moment he spotted the cows at the other end of the pen, Dudley perked up even more. That didn't mean he lifted his head. No, his horse dropped it, like a jungle cat sighting prey, and that was an apt analogy because Dudley really did think of the cows as his prey.

Baldy, black body. Where was it? The first rider he'd watched had had a pretty good run cutting it out of the herd. He spotted it near the back, just to the right of one of the two men holding the herd in place. Perfect. Competitors had to cut at least one of their cows "deep," meaning no pulling a cow from the edges. Points were deducted if you gave up on a cow—or a miss—or if your cow ducked out on you and made it back to the herd.

The black cow seemed to know the jig was up. The animal tried to move away, but Dudley knew his quarry, committing to the small black cow with a minimal amount of urging on Wes's part. It couldn't go very fast, surrounded as it was by other animals. Neither could Dudley. Too fast and he'd scatter the herd like a cue ball did a rack of pool balls. Dudley did just as he was supposed to do, walking near the cow's hip, slowly edging the animal away from the back fence and out into the open. The moment the cow sensed freedom, though, it broke away. Wes didn't have to do a thing. Dudley bolted after it as if there were carrots taped to its tail. In a matter of seconds they had the animal separated from the herd.

Game on.

It was as Jillian said. Dudley loved the audience. The claps. The cries. The calls. Wes didn't know why he had a silly grin on his face. All he knew was a sense of awe as his little colt swung from side to side, ears pinned back, front end low to the ground as he held the cow away from the herd. Left, right. Left, right. One quick run toward the in gate when the cow bolted. Dudley cut him off, then held him perfectly in the center of the ring. He was having a good run, but inside his head a timer went off. He needed to cut a total of two cows, maybe even three if there was time. Wes picked up his reins, a signal for Dudley to quit. The black baldy sped off, happy to return to its pals, tail flicking, ears pinned back.

Which one next? Wes drew a blank. Dudley made the decision for him. A brindle calf tucked off to the left. With little to no guidance his horse cut the cow out of the herd. Once again they held it on the opposite wall. Wes would remember nothing about that cow.

His brain switched on for the third and final cow. There'd been a Charolais in the herd—off-white with some brown around the flank—easy to spot, and a real handful. If he could find it...

There.

He spotted it deep. Not necessarily a bad thing, but

he might be running out of time. No way to look at the clock. He rode on pure instinct now. He would have to cut it from the herd quickly. No time for a mistake. No time for a miss. No second chances.

The damn cow didn't make it easy.

He should have expected that. From what he'd seen earlier the cow had the potential to be either really good or really bad. Wes was on the verge of thinking he'd made a mistake, the cow rearing up in the middle of the herd at one point and switching directions. Dudley never missed a step. He had no idea how his horse knew which cow he wanted, but that was what it felt like, as though Dudley read his mind. He'd never experienced anything like it. Good thing, too, because that little cow took off like a house on fire the moment they pushed it away from its buddies. Dudley took off, too. One leap, two, three—his little horse cut the animal off, turning it back. This wasn't good, Wes thought. They needed to hold the animal in the middle of the pen, not chase it around. Once again he wondered if he'd blown it, if perhaps he'd picked the wrong cow, but no sooner did he have the thought than the cow stopped. Dudley froze, turned, faced her, and there it was. The dance. The waltz. Like having an ice-skating partner or facing a mirror—that was what a good run felt like. Everything the cow did, Dudley did, too. Every duck, every run, every stop. When the buzzer sounded, Wes almost collapsed onto his horse's neck. Instead, he bent and patted his neck so hard he could hear the clap of his palm.

Wait.

That was clapping from the crowd. As he came up for air, he realized everyone was hooting and hollering.

For him. For Dudley.

Chapter Twenty-One

"What happened?" Jillian faced her friends. "Was that good?"

"That was remarkable," Vivian said, standing up with a glance down at the baby in her stroller. "That last run was textbook clean. Amazing."

Oh, thank God.

She hadn't breathed the entire time—or so it seemed. "What did he score?"

Mariah shook her head at her excitement. "We'll have to watch a few more goes before we know."

Oh, yeah. That's right.

"I'm going to go see him," Vivian said. "Will someone watch the baby?"

"Zach and I will watch her," Mariah offered. "Jillian, you go, too. After all, none of this would have been possible without you."

Should she? She'd done what she'd come to do. She'd watched Wes. She'd helped with Dudley, too, or so she hoped, but there was no way to know for certain if the calming thoughts she'd sent him while he was in the pen had done any good.

"Come, dear," Vivian ordered. "I want to catch him as he leaves the arena."

A glance toward the exit revealed Wes had ridden toward the out gate. The competitor replacing him said something as they passed each other. She couldn't see Wes's face, but the way he patted Dudley's neck told Jillian Wes was pleased by whatever the man had said. She got up before she could think better of it and followed Vivian as she hopped down from the grandstands like someone half her age. Jillian watched as Vivian caught up with her son first. He had a grin on his face that stretched from ear to ear.

"That was perfect." She heard Vivian say, patting Wes's leg so hard Jillian winced.

"You think so?" Wes bent and gave his mom a hug. "It felt good."

"It *was* good."

"I can't believe how great he was." Wes's gaze moved past his mom as if searching for someone. When he spotted her, the pride in his eyes and the smile on his face somehow grew even more. Her heart went *plunk* all over again.

"You did it," she said softly, wanting so badly to hug him, too.

"We did it," he said. "Although nothing's for certain. The judges might think differently."

"Was it scary?"

"Terrifying." His eyes grew serious for a moment. "But overcoming that fear makes victory all the sweeter."

She swallowed hard. He was talking about her... talking about *them*.

"Wes, I—"

"Good job!" a voice boomed, Jillian just about jumping. A heavyset man with a straw cowboy hat stood behind her. "That was one amazing run." The man reached out and patted Dudley's sweaty neck. "Looks like a good little horse. Who'd you buy him from?"

Wes seemed a little thunderstruck as he stared down at the man. "We found him at the bull-and-gelding sale in Red Bluff a few months ago."

"You're kidding? Who was he trained by?"

"Hadn't had much training before he came to me."

"You a professional?"

"I am, but I mostly ride for other trainers, and I have another horse. Been doing some winning on him this past year."

"That's right," the man said, snapping. "I've seen you riding a bay."

"Bugs in My Chex."

"That's him." The man laughed. "I remember the name. Funny. And another nice horse. Are you riding Bugs in My Chex today, too?"

"No, sir." He tipped his hat back. "He bowed a tendon over the winter."

"Aww, too bad. You interested in talking about selling this one?"

Wes's mouth dropped open for a second. "Well, I... Sure. I guess everything's for sale."

"If the price is right, it usually is, and I'm not known for lowballing trainers. Mike McCutcheon." He held out his hand.

Wes took it. "I know who you are, sir."

"You mind if we talk for a moment?" He scanned the area, clearly looking for a place where they could be in private instead of by the always-busy gate.

Jillian caught Vivian's gaze. She looked ready to cry.

"Do you know who that man is?" she said as the two of them walked away.

Jillian shook her head, the sight of Vivian's tears—happy tears, she realized—causing her own eyes to burn. "I have no clue."

"He owns some of the best cutting horses in the business. He wouldn't be talking to Wes if he wasn't serious about making him an offer, and after the go Wes just had, it'll be a lot of money."

"But we don't even know how he scored."

Now Vivian shook her head, a smile slowly creeping up her face, her eyes glittering. "It doesn't matter. It's what he's capable of. Anyone who knows anything about cutting horses knows Dudley's going to be a star." Vivian looked amazed. "Do you know what this means? It doesn't matter what Wes scores today. He's going to make the last bit of money he needs. No matter what. Either with prize money or with the sale of Dudley, although I hope it's prize money. I kind of like that little horse. Wish I could buy him myself."

The speakers popped. Vivian and Jillian froze.

"We have the score for entry 1550. Judges mark a seventy-nine."

"Hah!" Vivian cried. "Hah, hah, hah." She turned and tried to catch her son's eye. He must have heard, because he reached down and patted his horse's neck, a wide smile on his face.

"Do you think he'll win?"

"I don't know, but he'll be in the money."

So he'd done it. As Vivian said, one way or another. Even if he didn't have the top score of the day, he would still be okay. He'd earned his right to own Landon Farms.

"Tell him congratulations."

She needed to get away, although why, she couldn't articulate. Her heart had started to pound as she turned away.

"Wait. Where are you going?" Vivian asked.

Jillian waved. "Looks like Wes will be a while." She forced a smile. "And I need to get something to eat. I'll be back."

She had to come back. She needed a ride home. It was just that seeing him sitting there, all his dreams having come true, it hurt for some reason. Was she jealous? No. She couldn't be more thrilled for him. Yet she needed to avoid him. She almost laughed. Who was she kidding? She'd been avoiding him for weeks.

Overcoming that fear makes victory all the sweeter.

He'd been talking right at her. And after the way he'd been smiling at her earlier, and the look in his eyes when he'd come out of the ring, she knew he still had feelings. He didn't hate her.

So?

They were friends. They were still friends. They would always be friends.

Except suddenly, she wanted more. She longed for it with a keening pain that was almost physical.

She quickly wiped her eyes, embarrassed by her tears. There were people around. People walking. People riding. People driving around in golf carts. She clutched her hands to her stomach. It wasn't just the pain in her gut; it was her heart. It beat so quickly and so harshly that it felt as though she couldn't breathe.

It's your own damn fault.

That little voice again. The one that had called her ten times a fool for being afraid to fall in love with Wes. He was perfect in every way—and she had never believed in a perfect man. But Wes was as close to perfect as a man could get. He was the best. Kind to animals. Good to his mom. A hard worker. The ideal man—and she knew, she just knew, if she fell for him, life would never be the same. She'd spend the rest of her life scared to death that something would take him away. And not just Wes. What about Maggie? Hell, if she were being completely honest with herself, she was more afraid of assuming the role of mom than she was of falling in love with Wes. What if she let his little girl down? What if it turned out she was better with animals than she was with people?

A dog barked. Jillian swiped at her eyes. A dog barked again, closer this time, and there was another sound, a clippity-clop that was unmistakable. The sound of a horse running.

She turned.

Wes.

He rode toward her, hell-bent for leather, scandalized looks following in his wake, and out in front of him, Cowboy. She stood there, frozen, wondering what he was doing. They were going to boot him from the show grounds for turning his dog loose and for running like that. And then he was close enough that she could see into his eyes, and she knew, she just knew what he was going to do.

"Wes, no."

Cowboy reached her first, jumping up on her. She almost fell. It knocked her off balance so that when Wes rode up alongside of her, she was still unsteady, which made it easy for him to bend down and hook her around the waist.

"Wes!"

Cowboy barked. People stared. Someone yelled. Wes ignored them all, just tugged her up in front of him and pulled her into his arms, and she knew it was over. All her fighting. All the distance she'd put between them. All the time she'd kept away from Landon Farms. *Pfft.* That was where it went. Out the door, because the moment Wes Landon held her, she was lost.

"Damn you," she said, trying to wiggle away. "I told you to stay away."

"No."

"I'm warning you, Wes, I'll scream."

"No, you won't."

"Yes, I will."

"Not if I kiss you."

"You will not—"

He kissed her. Her indignation lasted about 2.1 seconds. That was all it took. One more kiss. One more time of tasting him, of breathing him in, of being near his amazing goodness. It tipped her over the edge and she knew she'd kidded herself. She could resist no longer. She loved this man. Loved him with every fiber of her being.

She released a sob. He must have heard it, because he drew back. "What is it, love? Why are you crying?"

"Damn you," she said. "Damn you all to hell, Wes Landon."

Somehow he juggled the reins and her and his horse and yet managed to lift a hand to wipe away her tears. "Sometimes the thing we fear most is the thing we want most in the world."

She sucked in a breath, one that released tears for some reason. "Will you stop going all Dalai Lama on me?"

"It's true, though, isn't it?"

The kindness in his green eyes proved to be her undoing. "I love you."

"I know."

She drew back.

He kissed her again. Someone let out a woof of approval. Jillian hardly noticed. She was too busy letting go of it all. Her fears. Her insecurity. Her self-doubt. She admitted in that moment that with Wes by her side all things were possible.

"I love you," she repeated against his lips, her hands finding his cheeks. "I love you so much, Wes."

He leaned back, one side of his mouth tipping up in a smile. "You're just after my money."

She laughed. She couldn't seem to stop herself. Suddenly she was laughing and hugging him and kissing him again and she realized perhaps being in love wasn't such a scary thing after all.

Epilogue

The day of the wedding dawned beautiful and bright. In one of the upstairs rooms of Vivian Landon's stately home, the bride checked her appearance in the mirror once again.

"You look amazing."

Mariah Stewart, soon to be Mariah Johnson, turned away from her reflection, used both hands to adjust her breasts—one for each hand—and said, "Not bad, if I do say so myself."

Jillian tried not to laugh. But she was right. Her friend looked like a million bucks.

"I really thought white would bleach me out, but I guess I was wrong."

"It's your hair." Jillian pointed to the upswept do. "You could never be washed out with all that red hair."

Somehow they'd managed to tame it today. It was piled atop her head, allowing for the column of her neck to be exposed, and her shoulders, too. She wore a strapless gown, one with a skintight waist and flared skirt. She never would have figured her best friend would go for rhinestones and pearls, but she'd gone all out with her wedding gown. She glittered like a disco ball—

a thought that Jillian kept to herself because nothing could outsparkle the joy in her eyes.

"Wait until you and Wes get married."

Jillian glanced down at the diamond ring she wore, and as they always did, her eyes warmed when she looked at the two-carat stone. It had been Vivian's. Her future mother-in-law had cried her eyes out when Wes had slipped it on her finger two months after winning the Million Dollar Futurity.

"I'm counting the days," Jillian admitted. "Although it should be easy to follow in your footsteps. You did all the work figuring out where to put everything in Vivian's backyard."

"That's not a backyard—that's a football stadium disguised as a backyard."

"And a good thing, too. Half of the racing world is out there. I just hope a riot won't break out when our friends from CEASE figure out they're sitting next to an evil racehorse owner."

Mariah smiled, but whatever she'd been about to say was interrupted as Natalie burst into the room. "They're ready for us," she gushed. "And I think—" She gasped. "Oh, Mariah. You look…" She shook her head, tears coming to her eyes. "You look amazing."

"You think?"

"You do." Natalie's gaze fell on the flowers. "Here." She handed Jillian her maid-of-honor bouquet, a tussie-mussie of white roses, baby's breath and lemon sprigs, then grabbed her own. "All the groomsmen are downstairs, waiting for us. I tried to get that moron Colton Reynolds to take off his cowboy hat, but he insists on wearing it. I swear, Mariah, that man's an ass."

"That man's one of the most famous rodeo perform-ers around."

"Yeah, well, I'll have to take your word for it. I, for one, wouldn't be able to stand watching him for even five seconds."

"Are you ready?" Jillian asked as Mariah took an even bigger bouquet from Natalie.

"As I'll ever be."

Natalie stepped back, her gaze sweeping Mariah up and down.

"Perfect," she said before turning and leaving the room.

Jillian helped Mariah lower an ivory veil, then darted around the back of her friend, making sure her train didn't catch on any of Vivian's furniture. Down the steps into the massive foyer they carefully trod, pass-ing by the living room where Vivian had tried to tell her not to be afraid and then to the back door, where she paused while Natalie opened the door.

"Here we go."

Mariah glided onto an ivory-colored runner that led down the pathway of Vivian's tiered backyard, where wedding guests sat in chairs on each level, and to an altar in a garden area down below.

"Beautiful," she heard her friend whisper. "Just per-fect."

When she slipped through the doors, her gaze scanned the group of men standing outside. She found Wes al-most immediately. He was Zach's best man, which meant they would walk down the aisle together, not for the last time, and he couldn't have looked more dashing in his black tuxedo and cowboy boots.

"I'll see you after," Jillian said to Mariah as she hooked her arm through her perfect groom's.

Mariah stood next to her dad, a man with a shock of hair as red as Mariah's, waving her forward. Jillian glanced up at Wes as they began their walk. He leaned down close to her ear and whispered, "Don't tell the bride, but you're the prettiest thing here."

"Pfft." She shook her head, but not before returning his smile. "Not possible. I swear I'm going to make Mariah wear a pumpkin-orange dress when *we* get married."

Okay, maybe it wasn't that bad, but pink was *not* her favorite color. It looked great on Natalie. Then again, her blonde friend would look like a million bucks in duct tape and camouflage. Not so for Jillian. At least it was a summer dress, though, a sleeveless bodice with an ankle-length skirt. It was the color that bothered her most. *Pink*. Ugh.

"You look gorgeous."

She shook her head, but they were halfway down the aisle and up ahead sat Vivian, Maggie in her lap and looking absolutely adorable in a matching pink dress, a wreath of flowers on her head. She was a flower girl today, although she was a little too young to be on official duty. Cowboy, too, had been invited to the wedding. The dog looked ashamed of the big pink bow tied around his neck, although his tail thumped when he spied the two of them. Vivian lifted the baby's hand as they approached as if making her wave, and Jillian couldn't help but smile even more. The little girl had taken over a permanent spot in her heart. She loved her as if she were her own, although Maxine still had custody of her from time to time. Wes had full custody, though, and that was good because Maxine had quickly resumed her party-girl lifestyle. Thank God the little girl had Wes. Thank God they *both* had Wes. It hadn't taken Jillian long to admit she'd been a fool to fight off falling in love. You couldn't fight fate, and she had no doubt she and Wes were meant for each other.

"See you after." Wes echoed her own words. She nodded, smiled at Zach, who stood near the altar, and then turned to face the crowd just as the bridal march started, and though she'd told herself she wouldn't cry, she found herself close to tears as she watched her best friend pause at the top of the steps. A summer breeze caught the edge of her veil, pressing it against her face. She no longer looked like a disco ball. Instead, she resembled a heavenly angel, one who'd fallen from the stars to land in their midst.

"Damn," she thought she heard Zach whisper.

Mr. Stewart handed his daughter off, but not before lifting her veil and kissing her. Mariah, too, seemed on the verge of tears as she leaned in close to her dad, glanced behind him to her mom sitting opposite Vivian, then locked gazes with her groom. Jillian saw her take a deep, shaky breath, her eyes full of pure joy as she walked to Zach's side.

So much for not crying.

The ceremony passed quickly. Wes and Mariah had opted for the quickie version—or so the pastor had called it. It seemed Jillian blinked and the pastor was saying Zach could kiss his bride. With a whoop and a holler that startled baby Maggie into crying, Zach and Mariah kissed like a couple in a romantic movie.

"Ladies and gentlemen," the pastor announced, "may I present Mr. and Mrs. Zachary Johnson."

And there went the tears again, this time because of the look of pride on Zach's face and the answering expression of love on Mariah's face. It made Jillian's breath catch. Did she look at Wes like that? Did Wes look at her like that? She had a feeling they did.

Wes must have been thinking the same thing. "Our turn next," he whispered as they followed in Zach and Mariah's wake. "If you don't chicken out on me."

"You're never going to let me live that down, are you?"

He leaned back and smiled. "Never."

She didn't blame him. She'd been an idiot. Wes had compared her to a timid mare, one who'd been afraid of her own shadow. It had taken a gentle hand to tame her and to teach her to trust in his kindness, but eventually she'd learned to accept love. She wasn't so sure she liked being compared to a horse, but it was an apt analogy.

"You know what?" Wes said as they reached the top terrace. "I think you're right. I think that dress looks terrible on you."

"Wes!"

"In fact, I think I'm going to have to rip it off you right now." She giggled. He tugged her around and into his arms. "But first I think I need to kiss you."

He did exactly that, and even though Mariah and Zach's wedding guests were no doubt watching, she didn't care, because it was his kiss that reminded Jillian that she had nothing to fear. In his kiss she found not just love but courage, the courage to face a wild world, a world made just a little less crazy by Wes and his daughter and his mother—her family. Her *new* family.

"I love you," she whispered against his lips.

His kissed her back, gently, softly, before teasing her. "Are you sure?"

"Positive."

"Good, because I'm not going anywhere, Jillian Thacker."

She rested her head in the crook of his neck. "I know."

"Not ever."

She leaned back. "I know."

And she did know. And she was right about him never leaving her side. It was a promise he did keep—a promise they *both* kept—forever.

* * * * *

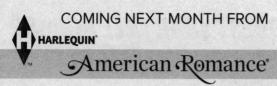

REQUEST YOUR FREE BOOKS!
2 FREE NOVELS PLUS 2 FREE GIFTS!

HARLEQUIN

American ★ Romance®

LOVE, HOME & HAPPINESS

Ryder stood at the pasture fence, his leather dress shoes
sinking into the soft dirt. He'd have a chore cleaning them
later. At the moment, he didn't care.

When, he absently wondered, was the last time he'd
worn a pair of boots? Or ridden a horse, for that matter?
The answer came quickly. Five years ago. He'd sworn then
and there he'd never set sight on Reckless again.

Recent events had altered the circumstance of his
enduring disagreement with his family. Liberty, the one
most hurt by their mother's lies, had managed to make
peace with both their parents. Not so Ryder. His anger had
not dimmed one bit.

Was coming home a mistake? Only time would tell. In
any case, he wasn't staying long.

In the pasture, a woman haltered a large black pony and
led it slowly toward the gate. Ryder leaned his forearms on
the top fence railing. Even at this distance, he could tell two
things: the pony was severely lame, and the woman was
spectacularly attractive.

The pair was a study in contrast. While the pony hobbled
painfully, favoring its front left foot, the woman moved with
elegance and grace, her long black hair misbehaving in the

mild breeze. She stopped frequently to check on the pony, and when she did, rested her hand affectionately on its sleek neck.

Something about her struck a familiar, but elusive, chord with him. A memory teased at the fringes of his mind, just out of reach.

As he watched, the knots of tension residing in his shoulders relaxed. That was, until she changed direction and headed toward him. Then he immediately perked up, and his senses went on high alert.

"Hi," she said as she approached. "Can I help you?"

She was even prettier up close. Large, dark eyes analyzed him with unapologetic interest from a model-perfect oval face. Her full mouth stretched into a warm smile impossible not to return. The red T-shirt tucked into a pair of well-worn jeans emphasized her long legs and slim waist.

"I'm meeting someone." He didn't add that he was now ten minutes late or that the someone was, in fact, his father.

"Can I show you the way?"

"Thanks. I already know it."

"You've been here before?"

"You…could say that. But it's been a while."

Look for HER RODEO MAN by New York Times bestselling author Cathy McDavid, available March 2015 wherever Harlequin American Romance books and ebooks are sold!

www.Harlequin.com

HARLEQUIN®

A *Romance* FOR EVERY MOOD™

Stay up-to-date on all your
romance-reading news with the
Harlequin Shopping Guide,
featuring bestselling authors, exciting new
miniseries, books to watch and more!

The newest issue will be delivered right to you
with our compliments! There are 4 each year.

Signing up is easy.

EMAIL

ShoppingGuide@Harlequin.ca

WRITE TO US

HARLEQUIN BOOKS
Attention: Customer Service Department
P.O. Box 9057, Buffalo, NY 14269-9057

OR PHONE

1-800-873-8635 in the United States
1-888-343-9777 in Canada

Please allow 4-6 weeks for delivery of the first issue by mail.